RANGER PRIDE

BROTHERHOOD PROTECTORS WORLD

LAYLA CHASE

Twisted Page Press LLC

BROTHERHOOD PROTECTORS

ORIGINAL SERIES BY ELLE JAMES

ACKNOWLEDGMENTS

Thanks to cover artist, Tamra Westberry, for another great cover.

Thanks to Shenoa Carroll-Bradd from LustreEditing.com for her story insights and copy editing.

In some small way, I hope to honor the dedication and service of all military dog handlers and their canine teammates—past, present and future—with this story.

CHAPTER 1

CRYSTAL-CLEAR WATER LIT by sunrays that cut the surface. I float weightless among colorful fish, shimmering in lazy patterns. Tiny disruptions chop the waves. Bullets pierce the calm area where I float. The fish jerk and scatter. Concussions of rapid fire surround me. Fear of being struck freezes me immobile. A torturous bang rattles my brain then I sink toward the depths…

A warm, wet lick slurped from his nose to his ear. Throwing off the sheet, Beck sat upright in his bed and drew the back of a hand across his stubbled cheek. His heart thundered in his chest. "Ugh." He pried open his eyes and glanced at the German Shepherd, bracing front paws on the mattress edge. "King, sitta."

The dog dropped to all fours on the carpeted floor before lowering onto his haunches, gaze glued to the man in bed.

Beck ran a hand over his face then squinted against the bright sunlight streaming through the window. Damn, overslept again. Sleeping with his undamaged ear buried in the pillow meant he heard almost nothing, maybe ten percent of any exterior noise. The diagnosis was hard to digest, and he clung to the hope his hearing would return.

With a whine, King scratched a paw on the mattress.

"Yeah, right. I'm up." Beck shoved to his feet, grabbed a pair of camo pants from where he'd dropped them the night before, and pulled them over his hips. King was a couple hours past due for being outside. As soon as Beck opened the bedroom door, he smelled brewed coffee. His roommate and landlord, Tag, must be up and about.

King remained right where he'd settled, ears pointed forward.

The training continued, even if he and King didn't have specific tasks. "King, fri." Beck stood to the side, watching the Shepherd scamper from the room. Then he walked to the kitchen and checked the yard to make sure Tag wasn't running a dog training class before opening the back door.

King shot outside and raced to lift a leg on the nearest fence post.

Yawning, Beck tipped back his head and gazed at the blue sky marked by a handful of clumpy clouds. Sure never saw views of rugged mountains on the horizon in the Nebraska corn fields where he'd grown up.

The warming morning air felt good on his skin. He scratched a hand across his bare chest, fingers lingering over the rough scar above his right pec. Another souvenir from the team's last mission. Four months earlier, when he'd been medically discharged from the army due to profound hearing loss, he hadn't known where to go. Or what he'd do after almost a decade in the military, the last four years working with bomb-sniffing dogs.

A phone call from Tag Redmond, a Ranger he'd gone through military dog handler training with, had provided a roof over his head and a possible way back into civilian life. Tag had convinced Hank Patterson, his boss at Brotherhood Protectors, that ex-military dogs would be a great addition to the private security service. Especially canines with explosive-sniffing abilities.

Problem was, now that Beck and King had been here in Eagle Rock, Montana, for a couple months, he couldn't get King to reengage in tracking work. He and Tag had worked King through the drills they'd learned at Lackland Air Force Base, but King wouldn't budge from Beck's side.

Beck moved to the counter and reached down a ceramic mug for his first cup of coffee. Before taking a sip, he angled his head in all directions, listening. No sounds came from any other part of the house. Wonder where Tag is today. Probably somewhere with his lady, Malin.

Thirty minutes later, Beck jogged in the forest at the back side of Tag's property. The late August air was hot enough to raise a sweat on his exposed shoulders. King followed close at his heels, and they moved under a canopy of red cedar, larch, and pine trees. Running without a thirty-pound pack on his back still felt strange. But a daily run at almost five thousand feet elevation taxed his body in different ways.

Ahead, a jackrabbit dashed under a honeysuckle bush.

King sprang after the animal, burying his nose deep into the pink and white flowers on the shrub. "Ai-aiyee!" The shepherd howled and rolled on the ground, rubbing a paw over his muzzle.

After a moment of staring, slack-jawed, at his dog who'd broke all training protocols, Beck ran close and dropped to his knees. He rested a hand on King's shoulder. Angry bees buzzed, and he stilled, waiting for them to settle. Already, the skin along King's lip had puffed. Beck stood and snapped his fingers. "King, häl. Komma." He trained with Swedish commands so King would mind only him in the worst and most dangerous situations. He dug out his cell phone from his shorts pocket. "King, häl."

Head low, King complied and trotted behind.

As he fast walked, he punched words into the keyboard then scrolled through the listings, looking for a local address for a veterinarian who handled walk-ins. Dr. Whitaker listed by appointment only. Gallatin Animal Hospital was more than twenty miles away. Crazy Mountain Rescue, just outside of Eagle Rock, handled emergencies. That's the one. After a ruffle of King's ears, he grabbed jeans and a T-shirt before heading into the bathroom to rinse off the sweat and grime.

When Beck loaded his dog into his pick-up, he noticed King kept shaking his head. On the road heading south out of Eagle Rock, he barely kept under the speed limit. Thankfully, the rescue facility was easy enough to find. A gray, two-story farmhouse sat a hundred feet or so off the road with white-painted rail fencing marking the border of a big back yard. Colorful curtains on an upstairs window indicated the vet probably lived on premises.

Beck clipped a lead onto King's collar then led him through the front door into what once must have been the living room. A hallway disappeared down the left exterior wall, and two doors were positioned about eight feet apart along the wall behind the reception area. The silhouette of a cat adorned one door with a dog on the other.

"Hello. How can I help you?" A dark blonde-haired woman wearing a pink shirt printed with dogs and cats spoke from behind a short counter.

On a shelf behind her, a bird with a bandaged wing sat at the bottom of a cage.

"My dog suffered bee stings. I don't know how many but his lip is swelling fast." Beck leaned his right elbow on the counter, made eye contact with his dog, and pointed to the ground next to his feet. "I need the doctor to take a look."

Brow wrinkled, King sat and watched him, head tilted. At this point, the lip on his right side swelled enough to expose the tips of his teeth. His tongue lolled from the side of his mouth.

Beck couldn't be sure, but he thought his dog's breathing sounded raspier.

"I know you haven't been here before, or I'd have remembered." As she handed him a clipboard, she flashed a dimpled smile.

Beck focused on the printed form so he didn't have to acknowledge the interest he heard in her voice. Until he got his life in order, he had no intention of dating. Only with great effort did he keep from making sure the hair over the top of his left ear covered the hearing aid he wasn't yet used to wearing. "Yep, I'm new in the area."

He grabbed a pen from the cup on the counter and walked over to a plastic chair. Damn, he should have collected King's shot record from their discharge papers. From memory, he filled out what he could then double-checked his phone for Tag's number to list as emergency contact.

After returning the clipboard, he walked the perimeter of the small space. On the wall hung photos of a dark-haired, smiling woman with several species of animals, including a goat, a lamb, a couple horses, and a multitude of dogs and cats. In each photo, she touched the animal with what looked like a caring hand. He imagined strokes bestowed by those long fingers being languid and soothing.

"Mr. Gunnar, bring King this way, please."

He nodded, stooped to collect King's lead, and led him to where the assistant stood next to a scale.

"Have King step on the platform."

Beck followed her direction, gave the hand signal for sit. "Huh, he's lost five pounds since our last weigh-in." Another sign his canine buddy wasn't back to his old self.

"Okay, I'll note that for the doc." She waved a hand toward the dog-designated door. "Right through here. Dr. Orestes will be with you shortly."

As he walked them into a small examination room, Beck noted the pressure of King's shoulder on his calf. He settled into a chair and dropped the lead, listening to the dog's heavy breathing. That sound is not normal.

King belly-crawled to work his way under an adjoining chair and positioned himself between Beck's shoes, facing outward.

Not an easy feat for a seventy-pound dog. When the team had traveled to missions—in planes, helicopters, trucks, or cars—King was trained to stay close. Often, having the canine between the handler's feet was the best way to keep the dog safe. Resting his elbows on his knees, Beck let his fingers dangle and sift through King's thick brown-and-black fur. On the opposite wall hung a framed certificate...probably a license. A diagonal crack ran through the glass. Odd. Everything else about the room was in neat order.

The door whooshed open, and in walked the slim woman from the photos, her wavy hair pulled into a high ponytail. "Hello, Mr. Gunnar. I'm Dr. Orestes." She stopped at the edge of the metal examination table and extended a hand, her gaze flicking between the room's occupants.

The lady vet was even better-looking in person. Her dark eyes sparkled as she smiled at the man and dog team. He shot to his feet and clasped her hand. "Call me Beck." The firmness of her handshake surprised him, and the warmth of her touch proved hard to ignore. He stared, noting crinkles at the edges of her eyes that evidenced time spent outdoors.

"Now, where did this big beautiful guy get stung?" The doctor squatted, her attention on the hiding dog.

Beck inched to the side, unsure if he should command King to heel or if the doctor expected to forge her own relationship.

"You poor baby. Your swollen lip looks painful." She reached out a hand, fingertips down, and waited. When she got no response, she sat cross-legged opposite the dog.

Crooning, she complimented King on his amber eyes, muscular frame, and thick fur. Nonsense statements that had nothing to do with determining his ailment, but her calm tone permeated the air. Beck was just about ready to follow her anywhere.

King belly-crawled from his spot and rested his jaw on her knee. His reward was an ear scratch.

Slowly, she slipped a stethoscope from around her neck and pressed the silver disk against his rib cage. Angling her elbow upward, she glanced at her watch while still cupping fingers around his ear. "Hmm. I don't like the sound of his breathing."

So, he had been right. Beck forgot all about her soothing voice and pretty face. "What's wrong?" He dropped down to one knee and scratched his fingers along King's belly.

"Just like people, some animals are sensitive to bee venom. An intravenous antihistamine infusion will combat any constriction in his airway." As she explained, she ran her fingers through the fur along King's throat.

The dog relaxed enough to lie on his side, still panting.

Infusion. His gut clenched. Needles. "Sure, no problem."

"I'll want to observe him overnight."

"Whatever's necessary." Better you than me. He'd endured the requisite vaccinations and immunizations determined by the locations where his team might have been sent. But he always dreaded the experiences.

"Excuse me." The doctor unclipped a walkie-talkie

from her waistband and gave several precise instructions.

Almost before he knew what was happening, Beck watched a stocky male attendant slide a noose-like loop over King's head and lead him through the back door.

Beck stood, staring at the spot where his buddy disappeared. King didn't even glance back. Poor dog must be hurting more than Beck imagined. The pair hadn't been apart since Beck's hospital discharge. Not hearing the click of King's nails or feeling his weight against his leg disconcerted him.

"Will that time be convenient?" The doctor cocked her head, her brows pinched.

"Sorry, what?"

"One o'clock for a pick-up time." She smiled. "I realize you probably weren't expecting to leave him here, Mr. Gunnar."

"Beck, please." Something about this woman drew him. He hoped she'd take the hint to become better acquainted on a more personal basis.

"Only if you call me Danae."

The name sounded as elegant and different as she appeared with her olive skin and dark wavy hair. "You're right, Danae. I thought you'd give me some pills I'd have to hide in his food." He ran a hand down his face and looked to the side, afraid if he kept staring into her compassionate eyes he might start bawling. His gaze caught on the cracked certificate. "I could replace that glass, you know."

"Oh, no." Smiling, she shook her head. "I leave that hanging like my badge of courage. Or stupidity, I haven't decided which one."

"Gotta be a story there."

"That's my reminder not to underestimate the power of a wounded animal. On my first day, a client brought in a Great Dane with a tooth ache. I made the mistake of touching its face before restraining it and got knocked against the wall."

Her self-effacing tone relaxed him, and he returned her smile. He admired those individuals who admitted their mistakes.

A phone trilled.

Danae lifted a cell phone from her scrubs pocket and swiped a finger along the screen without glancing at it. "Hello, Dr. Orestes speaking." Her dark eyebrows bunched, and she angled her body toward the opposite wall.

If Beck hadn't been studying the intriguing woman, he might not have noticed the subtle signs of distress-- whitened knuckles, a hitch in her breathing, shoulders inching closer to her ears. He stiffened, his gaze narrowing on her tight expression.

"You are mistaken...I don't know what you're talking about. Please do not call again." After punching a finger at the screen, she jammed the phone toward her back pocket and missed.

"Is everything all right?"

A second passed before she took a deep breath and succeeded in replacing her phone. "Just a crank call."

Bullshit. "Really?" What made someone who had been so open and easygoing a moment ago just shut down?

She reached to a breast pocket for a pen, but her hand shook. "Uh huh." She flipped open the file folder and moved to the back counter to jot notes. Her left foot bounced against the vinyl floor.

All his senses were on alert. The lady doctor was really bothered. He stepped close, so she couldn't ignore him in her peripheral vision. Instinct told him he had the skills to help. Pride told him he might be the only one who could. Ego told him he wanted her calling him a big beautiful guy. "Tell me the truth."

CHAPTER 2

"Tell me the truth."

Spoken in his deep, resonating voice, the four words lured her to divulge her troubles. Something in this man's presence tempted Danae in ways she hadn't been enticed for a long time. She lifted her head and glanced into Beck's so-blue eyes that didn't blink or look away. A gaze that she would swear could see right through to her very soul.

The air between them heated, intensifying a faint scent of cedar and lime exuding from his body. But the man standing almost too close was a virtual stranger. Experience taught her the hard way not to let just anyone into her life.

His gaze narrowed, and he rolled his shoulders.

"The caller must have mixed me up with another person. Wrong numbers happen all the time." Shaking her head, she gave an exaggerated shrug, even though she'd recognized the rounded vowels of a Philadelphia accent.

Why would someone from back home taunt her? The smirking face of her ex-husband, Giles, surfaced, but she shoved away the distracting vision. Sure, he railed over the phone after being served with divorce papers. But he'd agreed to her proposed property settlement, allowing the final decree to be processed within three months. The online application was so austere compared to her elaborate wedding. But he and their disastrous mistake of a marriage were in her past.

Beck shifted his legs apart a couple inches and crossed muscled arms over his chest.

Okay, so Mr. Gunnar wasn't buying her explanation. If she hadn't seen this hunk of a man running bare-chested across a meadow less than an hour ago, Danae would have an easier time staying professional.

Refocusing on the folder, she jotted one more note, hoping to buy time. "I'm still processing an animal's death from earlier this morning." After euthanizing a dog left on the office doorstep, she'd needed just a few quiet minutes. Her solution consisted of grabbing the company's ATV and heading to one of her favorite spots overlooking a meandering creek. The poor little dachshund must have been struck by a car. Its piteous cries reached her second-floor bedroom and woke her right before dawn.

As best she could until her assistant arrived, she'd fought hard to repair its crushed chest, but the damage was too widespread. A lung had been punctured, and her skills and meager equipment didn't stretch to trauma surgery. Without a microchip or an identification tag providing owner details, she had little choice but to put down the suffering dog.

"That's tough." Beck didn't budge from his position, but the lines around his mouth eased. "Must be the hardest part of your job."

His compassionate tone wrapped around her jangled nerves. Savoring this tiny bit of empathy, she pressed a hip against the counter. "Almost." Around her employees, she always kept a positive attitude. The man standing only an arm's length away, with his broad shoulders and focused attention, looked like he could bear hearing what she normally hid bottled inside.

Right now, she yearned for a sympathetic ear. "The worst task breaks my heart every time when I inform the owners their pet either passed or suffers from an incurable disease. Their beloved pets are members of the family. Having to deliver the news they will never return or will never have the same quality of life takes getting used to." Her throat constricted, and she swallowed hard. "Everyone reacts differently. All the psychology courses in the world can't prepare anyone for facing such personal devastation. Every time, I hope the right words will come, but they never do."

"I hear what you're saying, Danae. No doubt, those circumstances are difficult. I don't look forward to facing a similar situation in the future." His gaze narrowed. "But the animal's death is not what distressed you during that phone call."

How could someone who'd met her only fifteen minutes earlier read her so well? Even after years of being together, Giles had been horrible at interpreting her body language.

A knock sounded before the back door opened a couple inches. "Sorry for the interruption, doc, but the infusion is set up and waiting."

Danae nodded at her dark-haired assistant. "I'll be right there, Eric." She pasted on a wide smile and pushed away from the counter to face Beck. "Duty calls, and I want to get that IV in place on King."

His forehead wrinkled, and he searched her expression for several seconds.

Being the object of such perusal kicked up her pulse. Attraction swirled low in her belly, and her nipples pearled. But the longer he stared, the more he reminded her of the overbearing men in her life she'd left behind in Philadelphia--her father, her ex-husband, and two older brothers. Them, she'd proved she could live without. Lifting her chin, Danae held the folder close to her chest, determined not to let her inner responses show.

Beck dropped his hands to his sides. "Agreed. Scratching base to tip on his ears calms him." Stepping back, he gave a curt nod. "I'll return tomorrow at thirteen hundred hours."

Watching him walk from the room with a definite swagger in his stride reminded her of the tanned, rippling muscles working in rhythm she glimpsed as he jogged with such precise movements. His use of a twenty-four hour clock confirmed her guess he served in the armed forces. No wonder she felt captured when his commanding gaze searched hers.

She grabbed the doorknob, ready to focus on the work that brought her joy. A different scenario for the word *joy* surfaced, diving into her lonely heart. Closing her eyes, she conjured intimate images of a certain light-haired, blue-eyed man hovering over her body. For just a moment, she basked in the sexy position of being the object of someone's intense attention.

Enjoying his strong hands caressing her body.

Enjoying his low voice whispering close to her ear.

Enjoying his warm breath feathering along her sensitive skin.

Her cheeks heated, and she swiped a hand over her suddenly damp forehead. Danae huffed out a long breath. Definitely not the way she should be thinking about a client.

At least, not during working hours.

Hours later following vaccinations, stitches, glands expressions, and foxtail removals, Danae flopped down behind the office desk and studied tomorrow's appointments on the calendar displayed on the computer monitor. Only four fifteen-minute slots were unclaimed. Emergencies or walk-ins would fill those spaces before ten o'clock. She leaned an elbow on the desk and took a bite of the banana that remained from her lunch. A sigh escaped.

Maybe she should schedule an occasional afternoon off so she could visit her friends, the Langstrom sisters, at Dream Vista Ranch. When was the last time she enjoyed one-on-one time with an animal instead of patching one up? Perhaps an invigorating horseback ride? Or an hour spent at Brighter Days Rehab Ranch always revived her spirits—even if the time there was like taking a busman's holiday. The rehabilitation work Hannah Davila conducted with animals and military veterans proved invaluable.

Danae let her gaze linger on the name typed into the box for one o'clock. Beck Gunnar—an interesting man. All afternoon, when she got a moment to catch her breath, he popped into her thoughts. On second, third, and ninth considerations, she'd changed her opinion about his bossy, take-charge attitude and found him endearing. Since she made the excruciating decision to defy her family's wishes and divorce Giles, she'd been adrift—without the familiar blockade of Greek relatives at her back.

The desk phone rang.

Danae glanced at the computer clock. Fifteen minutes past closing time. Should she answer the call or let it go to voicemail? If she didn't and someone needed emergency care, then they'd have the thirty-minute drive to Bozeman's twenty-four hour urgent care center. Her heart lurched at the thought of an animal in potential pain, and she lifted the receiver. "Crazy Mountain Rescue. Dr. Orestes here."

"Hey, Danae. It's Tilda. I probably should have called your cell phone."

"Hi, Tilda. Everything okay at Dream Vistas?" *Did the woman have E.S.P. or what?*

"People and animals are A-okay." She laughed. "And the guest ranch business keeps us busy. Thanks for asking."

Danae grinned and leaned back in the office chair, rotating her head to release tension. Her natural care-giver tendencies always occupied the forefront of her mind. "Good to hear. I was just pining over my last horseback ride, which must have been two months ago."

"At least. I've missed seeing you. In a few minutes, Jude and I will head over to the Blue Moose for a drink."

From the background came a shout. "And dancing. I need to shake my thing."

That would be the youngest Langstrom sister—Jude. Danae pictured the vivacious woman with white-blonde spiked hair. She giggled.

"Are you free to join us?"

After a day of tending animals and soothing

owners, Danae could use some downtime. "Drinks, for sure. Don't know about dancing. I've had a long day."

"We'll take what we can get. We're grabbing dinner here before we leave the ranch."

"I need to shower and scour my closet." She cringed at the image of the mountain of dirty clothes piled atop her laundry basket. "See you in thirty." She turned to the computer and clicked Print on tomorrow's schedule. Then she put the computer in sleep mode and dashed upstairs.

Thirty-seven minutes later, she pulled her SUV into a crowded tavern parking lot. Plenty of people here for a Wednesday night. She tightened her fingers on the steering wheel. *Hope Jude didn't rope me into a ladies' night or something.* As she walked through the door, she left the worries of her business behind. At the bar, she returned the acknowledging nod from Butch, the ever-present burly bartender.

Music filled the air from a three-piece group playing a popular country tune. She scanned the room, returned Annie's wave from the end of the bar, and noticed a few other townsfolk she had as clients. On the dance floor, she spotted Jude being twirled by a long-haired man who looked like he belonged in an artist's garret instead of a honky-tonk tavern. A movement at the corner of her eye spotlighted Tilda waving. Danae maneuvered right and left through the occupied tables, returning greetings to those who spoke, to drop into a chair opposite her smiling friend.

"Wow, you went all out."

"Not really." Danae glanced down at her lime green tank, low-waisted jeans topped with a big-buckled belt, and tooled leather boots then shrugged. "I checked into the dos and don'ts of cowgirl clothes after the teasing you three gave me on my first visit here. These are the last of the ones you haven't seen." She huffed out an exasperated breath and shook her head. "If my mother could see me now, she'd probably faint."

Tilda waved toward the pitcher in the middle of the table. "Help yourself to a beer."

"Thanks." Danae poured a mug full then swallowed, tasting the cool liquid accented with citrus. "Hmm, nice."

"So, your mom isn't a fan of jeans and boots." Tilda's green eyes sparkled over the rim of her mug.

"Hardly." Danae shook her head and laughed. Her family belonged to the elite in Philadelphia society, at least the merchant circles. "To Phedora, anything less than a designer label and stylish heels to bring in the mail is underdressed."

"I remember back east as being more of a dress-up place."

"Oh, that's right." The beer warmed her belly, and she tapped her foot to the music's snappy beat. "Your cousin, Caitlyn, told me your family used to live near her in St. Paul."

Smiling, Tilda nodded. "Yep, until I was fourteen."

The tune changed to a familiar line-dance.

"Now, that's more like it." Tilda jumped up and grabbed Danae's hand. "Let's get out there."

Danae tipped back her mug to finish her beer and followed. Stomping and kicking had been foreign steps when she arrived in Montana six months earlier. Now, she'd added her own shimmies and shakes to the dance's turns and slides. The music worked its magic and relaxed her like watching TV or reading couldn't. Dancing always made her smile.

When the music changed to a two-step, Danae turned toward the table but received a hip bump from Tilda.

"Don't look around, but Ryan Fletcher is headed this way, and his gaze is locked on you."

She gathered the bulk of her wavy hair with one hand and held it away from her damp neck. "Maybe he wants to dance with his boss."

"Not likely." Leaning close, Tilda spoke from behind her hand. "I intimidate the hell out of him." She let out a sigh. "Actually, being a boss must mark me, cuz no one from Eagle Rock ever asks me to dance."

Before she could assure her friend that wasn't the case, she heard a throat being cleared and turned toward the rough sound.

"Hey, Miss Danae. Care to dance?" The tall, dark-haired man extended a hand. The brim of his cowboy hat shaded his eyes.

Granted she was a few years older, but hearing him calling her 'miss' made her feel really old. She slipped her hand in his and allowed herself to be led to the wooden floor. "Sure, Ryan. But remember, I'm still learning so don't get too fancy."

"No worries. Everyone knows how to two-step." He swung her to face him and clasped her right hand in his left. "Don't look down."

As soon as she felt him grasp her shoulder blade, she settled into position and followed the six-beat rhythm of quick and slow steps leading them counter-clockwise around the floor. Thankfully, he always moved their joined hands toward the middle to signal a spin. Otherwise, she'd have tripped over her boots.

"Don't see you here often." He twirled her under his arm then pulled her back.

"My clinic and rescue work keep me pretty busy." Fighting not to look at her feet, she gazed over his right shoulder. Silently, she counted out the quick-quick-slow-slow steps.

"Too bad. I'd like to buy you a beer and get better acquainted sometime."

And there it came. The invitation she'd dreaded. Ryan was a nice enough guy who helped her saddle her horse when she rode at Dream Vista. But she never felt a single spark of interest. She shifted her gaze to look at his expression and stumbled. "Sorry."

"No problem." He glanced behind him.

The slight push against her hand signaled his first step and soon they were back in rhythm. They made a full circuit of the floor with spins for her and one for him without a single mistake.

When the music stopped, they stepped apart and clapped.

"Another?" His dark eyebrow cocked upward.

"I better get back to Tilda. Thanks, Ryan." Danae turned and sidestepped around a waiting couple, running smack into a solid body. "Oh, sorry."

"I'm not. You're looking real fine, Danae."

Strong hands reached to steady her elbows. The voice was familiar. She jerked her head upward, looking right into a direct blue-eyed gaze under a straw Stetson. Flutters invaded her chest. "Beck." To keep her balance, she rested both hands on his biceps. Warmth from his muscled arms seeped into her hands.

Violin strings twanged a long introductory note then the next number started.

Without a word, he slipped an arm around her waist and turned her toward the other dancers.

The dance position was the same as Ryan's, but every place Beck touched her body heated. She didn't have time to think about counting steps, because his expert contact nudged and tugged her into inside and outside turns, crossed their arms over the other's shoulders, and spun her away from him then reeled her close. All she could do was connect with his gaze and allow herself to be led through more complicated moves than she'd ever danced before.

When the tempo changed to a slow tune, without

even asking he snuggled her close and linked his hands at the small of her back.

Almost without thought, she clasped her hands around his neck and rested her head against his shoulder. Part of her wanted to protest because he commandeered the second dance. But being held in his arms felt too good, and they moved in perfect synchronization. A fact that reflected more on his ability as a strong leader than her talent. "Your dancing is quite accomplished."

"Not much else to do for entertainment in farming country."

"Where's that?" She eased back to glance into his face.

A hand cupped her head and lowered it back to his shoulder. "Your hair feels amazing against my hand. So thick."

Was he avoiding talking about himself? The slide of his thigh against hers shouldn't ignite such fire inside. And she relished the zing that coiled low in her belly. Her pulse already raced from the dances, but something more stirred. Hotter. More intimate. His shoulder cushioned her cheek, and she closed her eyes to savor all the physical sensations.

"King doing okay?"

He expects me to talk, too? "Uh, when I checked him around four he was."

"Swelling's gone down?"

At his mention of swelling, she realized her nipples

were budded and brushing him high on his tight abs. "Yeah." Crap, she sounded like a love-struck teen instead of a competent doctor. She lifted her head and moved a couple inches back from his enticing body. "The medicine did its job, and King should look normal when you see him next." A hard ridge nudged her inner thigh, and she bit back a sigh.

"Good to hear."

The violinist pulled a long, last note before the instruments silenced. "Folks, we're taking a fifteen-minute break. But don't go away, because we've got another set coming up."

Beck hooked a thumb inside her waistband, his fingers cupping her right hip.

"Have you got a table?"

Cheeks heating at the possessive gesture, she nodded. "I'm here with a couple friends. Come meet them." She waved a hand in the general direction while her mind raced, questioning if he treated other dance partners with the same intimacy. The thought disconcerted her. She tripped then stiffened at the hand braced low on her back.

As they neared the table, Danae watched Jude eyeing their approach with a widened stare. Danae's stomach clenched at what the outspoken, free spirit might say.

"Well, your dancing has certainly improved, lady D." Jude snaked out a long leg and claimed a chair from a nearby table, dragging it close.

"Jude and Tilda, this is Beck Gunnar. He brought his gorgeous German Shepherd in this morning with several bee stings. The poor thing needed IV meds." Now, why had she babbled about his pet's health? She angled her body so she could glance at Beck. "These ladies are two of the sisters who own and manage the Dream Vista Guest Ranch." She indicated with her hand as she repeated their names.

"Speaking of bees." Tilda held up Danae's black, cross-body bag. "Your phone has been buzzing like an agitated hive."

"Sorry about that." She dropped into an empty chair and fished into the inner pocket of her bag for her cell phone. Worrying about another crank call made her fingers jittery. When she grabbed it, Danae avoided connecting with Beck's gaze. The man was too perceptive, and she didn't want to ruin her enjoyable time.

Dimly aware someone slid a mug of beer in front of her, she lifted it to take a long swig. The screen showed three missed calls within fifteen minutes from her younger sister, Xenia. With a shrug, she glanced around the table. "I don't mean to be rude, but family…"

Jude waved a hand. "Say no more." Then she propped her chin in an upraised palm and stared. "Now, Beck, what's your story?"

As Danae typed a text to ask what was so important, she listened to the short version of his life. A childhood spent in the Midwest followed by ten years in the military, four years as a dog handler, and recently discharged.

Her phone pinged with a response. *Call me right now. Red-hot 911.*

An urgent emergency? She gasped and her throat tightened. Something bad must have happened. Illness? Injury? Her mind raced with the possibilities. "Sorry, I have to step outside and make a call."

Beck set down his mug and narrowed his gaze. "Let me escort you."

She jumped up and headed for the door. "Could I stop you?" As she walked through the crowded tables, she punched in her sister's number and waited. The call connected on the second ring. "Xenia, what's going on?" She angled her body away from the hovering male.

"Where are you?"

The urgency in Xenia's voice made Danae glance up at the Blue Moose sign. She and her parents weren't on the best of terms since her divorce six months earlier—an act they heartily disapproved of. In fact, they offered to pay for marriage counseling. But her suspicions about Giles and his business dealings weren't topics to compromise on. "At a tavern in Eagle Rock." After giving away her location, Danae winced. She couldn't remember if she'd revealed that fact yet. What she didn't need was a male Orestes swooping in and dragging her back to Philadelphia. "Why?"

"Someone broke into the house."

She gasped. Thoughts racing, she stiffened and stared unfocused at the ground. A warm hand rested on her shoulder. Her first instinct was to shrug it off, but the news set her stomach jumping. The reassurance she was here in the parking lot alone comforted her. "Anyone hurt?"

"Daddy shot at the intruder but missed."

"Since when does Father own a gun?"

"He bought it following the first time we were burglarized after you left." She cleared her throat. "The police say they targeted your room."

The first time? A shudder ran through her body. "My room? Why?"

Beck slid an arm around her back.

At that moment, resting her head on his broad shoulder felt like the most natural action. "I don't understand."

"We don't either, but I wanted to warn you to be careful."

Although she was more than two thousand miles away, Danae couldn't deny the uneasiness that swept through her. Why would someone break into her old bedroom?

CHAPTER 3

THE NEXT MORNING after his solo morning run, Beck drove his truck past the city limits of Eagle Rock and into the foothills of the Crazy Mountains. A call from Hank Patterson, the owner of Brotherhood Protectors security firm, first thing that morning spawned guilt over the lack of progress with King.

Before Beck's arrival, Tag advocated for trained dogs to be used as part of the protection services. Living under his friend's roof without producing the desired results didn't sit right. He figured Hank would be asking about a progress report, and Beck had no idea what he'd tell the ex-SEAL.

Tall cedars and pines bordered the winding road. Beck breathed the fresh scent deep into his lungs. Why the smell reminded him of Danae, he had no idea. Details of their interaction in front of the Blue Moose the previous night sifted through his mind. He'd wanted to offer much more than a listening ear. The irony of that phrase hit, and he tightened his grip on the steering wheel. Whatever banal words of comfort he'd muttered tasted like dust in his mouth.

The infuriating and independent woman hadn't shared more details after the phone call. Instead, she'd bid her friends a hasty goodnight and then dashed out of the parking lot.

Habits acquired from years of military service were hard to dismiss. He'd memorized the license number and important details about her silver SUV with paw print stickers in the rear window. A glance at her phone revealed she talked to someone outside of the immediate area. But where was this home located that attracted burglars?

The truck bumped through a pothole, and Beck jerked his attention back to the road. Wouldn't do to crash on the way to seeing his potential boss.

A few moments later, he steered into the clearing facing a sprawling, two-story cabin situated with the valley on one side and the rugged mountains on the other. *Nice digs.* Tag mentioned Hank's wife, Sadie, was a successful film star. Probably no expense had been spared when they rebuilt the house after Sadie's spiteful sister-in-law torched the family home.

Out of habit, Beck walked around the back of the truck to release King but stopped with a hand resting on the passenger door handle. The space inside held no waiting dog. He shook his head at letting thoughts of

Danae and her problem override the fact his dog was under her care. When had a woman messed with his mind like she did? Taking a deep breath to get his head straight, he headed toward the wide porch.

Hank pushed open the screen door. "Good to see you again, Beck."

Smiling, Beck extended his hand and accepted the man's strong shake. "Really like the drive here. Don't see mountains and trees like this back in Nebraska." The green was nice after spending the majority of the past decade in arid desert settings.

"Tag mentioned you were from the Midwest." The former SEAL led the way to his office.

Beck glanced around at the living room furnished with several couches and chairs accented with natural wood. His own adult existence had been such a vagabond lifestyle that he wondered if he'd ever acquire a home even half as spacious and well-situated.

"Take a seat. I'm anxious to hear about your progress."

A month had passed since their first discussion on the matter. Beck slipped into a chair facing the big desk where Hank sat in a high-backed executive chair. "Not as well as I'd hoped. We're still making adjustments."

"How so?" The dark-haired man steepled his fingers in front of his chin.

"Me, to not having a daily schedule and place to be by a certain time." Guilt stabbed him at the realization he had been living in a haze of pity over his injury.

"Him, to learning his new environment. That lightning and thunder storm we had last week set him back."

"I'll bet. I notice King's not with you today." The man's green-eyed gaze held solid.

"Yeah, that's an odd circumstance." Beck rubbed a hand over his chin. "He's at the vet's due to bee stings." An internal debate waged over revealing how King broke his training. When they were out together, the dog was supposed to remain right at Beck's side.

"Sorry to hear that." Hank leaned back and crossed his linked hands over his middle.

The man might have six or seven years on him, but he looked like he maintained a SEAL-readiness physique. Silence stretched, and Beck shifted in his chair. "I plan to ask the vet for a recommendation on re-engaging him in scent training."

"Good idea. From what I've heard, Doc Whitaker is experienced and should have a few pointers."

Should I have consulted with Hank about who to use? For all Beck knew, Hank already had an arrangement with place with the other veterinarian. Beck cleared his throat. "King's not with that doctor. He didn't take walk-ins, so King's being treated at the rescue facility south of town."

Hank's eyebrows crashed downward. "Oh." He reached forward and manipulated the computer mouse, his attention on the monitor. "The one operated by Danae Orestes?" He glanced back, his posture stiff.

Why would Hank have that information at his fingertips? Beck's senses alerted. Tag mentioned the man had contacts everywhere from his own military career. But Beck and King weren't officially connected to Brotherhood Protectors yet. "That's the one."

"And the exact reason for my call this morning. I received a request for services related to her this morning. Woke me up, in fact." He clicked a couple buttons, and the printer behind him whirred.

Echoes of Danae's side of the conversation from the previous night ran though his head. Beck sat forward, angling his body with his right side closer to the desk. "Related to the home invasion?"

"Nothing about an invasion was listed in the communication." Eyebrows winged high, Hank reached for the printed pages then slid them across the glossy desktop. "Even though the assignment wouldn't need dog-related services, I'd planned on seeing if you wanted the assignment. To get back into the action, so to speak. Sign this before our conversation can proceed. Confidentiality agreement about the potential case."

Hank shifted his attention back to the computer, typed for a few moments, and the printer started again. After the last page emerged, he tapped the stack even and stapled the upper corner. "The company's standard contract." He stood and set the papers on the desk. "I'm grabbing a cup of coffee. Do you want one or a bottle of water?"

Beck didn't look up from the document he scanned. "Black coffee's fine." *I'm really making this commitment?* The more he read, the more excited he became about being part of a team again. Even if this group was composed of guys working in one-on-one situations in scattered locations, a support system was in place. State-of-the-art equipment was supplied, and back-up could be called in at a moment's notice, including a helicopter. *Impressive.*

He grabbed a pen, signed his name on the last page, and filled in the date line. Although invisible, he'd taken a step forward in his life. The aroma of strong coffee preceded Hank's return.

"Here's yours."

Beck accepted the offered mug and sipped the rich brew.

After settling into the chair, Hank reached for the contract and glanced at the signature. "Good. Now tell me how in hell you already know about a burglary in Philadelphia."

Being in the know felt good. "I ran into Danae at the Blue Moose last night. You could say we hit it off." The memory of their sexy dancing warmed him from the inside out.

Looking over the rim of his mug, Hank rolled his hand.

"I was standing next to her when she got the news from what sounded like a sister. From what I over-heard, I believe the sister called from the premises."

"She did. Xenia Orestes is the woman who contacted me. My initial research revealed the Orestes are one of those families who keep their children close and enfold any spouses that pop up into the family business."

"Whoa. A crime family?" Beck thought of that phone call that Danae passed off as a wrong number. Were the two events connected?

"Not this one. Endre Orestes, the patriarch, has operated one of the most successful merchant shipping lines for the past thirty years. The company boasts customers from around the globe and is headquartered in Philadelphia."

Powerful men often crossed others in their business dealings. Disgruntled people often acted in inappropriate ways. But such a response should have been directed at the father, or the office complex—not personally toward Danae. Except, she mentioned her bedroom. "What's the scope of the requested security work?"

"Right now, we need to inform the lady security has been arranged. I intended to head over in a while to check out what security she has in place then consult about additional or upgraded cameras." He sipped his coffee. "Once the equipment is in, two drive-bys during the day and the program for her video feed will be installed on your computer as back-up monitoring. Basic first-tier actions. Since you already have a relationship, maybe this assignment is the perfect fit."

Beck set down his mug and leaned elbows on his thighs. "I'm scheduled to pick up King at one. We could show up together, and I'd learn your method for handling the situation."

Hank stood. "Good enough. Let's head to the basement and gather the basic equipment in case nothing is in place."

That he couldn't verify if he'd seen any cameras or even a security company sign on this visit to the rescue office showed just how out of practice at situational awareness he was. A factor he definitely needed to work on.

DURING THE PAST hour between treating animals, Danae glanced at her watch and the waiting room clock at least a dozen times. After last night, when Beck followed her home, she hadn't gone more than a few minutes without thinking about the sexy man. The way he stuck close when she walked outside to phone Xenia annoyed her at first. But she hadn't hesitated to lean on his quiet strength upon hearing the surprising news. An interesting action that she'd thought about for a long while before finally falling asleep.

Her stomach rumbled. One more task to finish before she grabbed her tuna sandwich and enjoyed a break on the back patio. She stood at the counter in the procedure room and typed notes into the permanent file for the overweight schnauzer she'd just examined.

The owner, Ruth Brandson, lifted her eyebrows almost into her coiffured bangs at the list of dietary and exercise recommendations. Only when Danae gently mentioned how obesity would shorten her precious Rocco's life had the woman changed her attitude.

Annie entered from the reception area, carrying a box of supplies. "Vera Simms wants to know if she can bring in Milo right away."

Danae glanced up, mentally reviewing the reason for today's visit. A feline panleukopenia booster shot. "An emergency?"

"No, she just remembered Bingo happens tonight in the Legion Hall. She booked a three o'clock hair appointment which conflicts with the one here." She sliced open the box and started loading prescription food cans into a lower cupboard.

So, the client's forgetfulness meant Danae had to cut her lunch break short? "Hmm." If she consented, would the pet owner expect similar a conciliation the next time, too?

"If you agree, then your afternoon is clear, because Earl Hanley moved Big Brute's exam to three-thirty tomorrow." Annie flashed a grin over her shoulder.

"Way to bury the lead. An afternoon off sounds great." She turned back to the monitor. "I can catch up on reading last month's professional journals."

"Or you could go upstairs, soak in a long bubble bath, and read a sexy romance novel." The receptionist flattened the empty box and hugged it against her chest.

"That suggestion sounds too decadent. I've got too much to do. But go ahead and tell Vera all right to the change."

"I already did." Annie winked and sashayed across the floor. "She'll be here in just a few minutes."

Danae stiffened and jammed a fist on her hip. "You told her yes without asking me?"

With a hand on the door jamb, Annie paused. "When have you ever said no to a client?"

Before she started sputtering, Danae slumped against the counter. Annie was right. Where the care of her furry clients was concerned, she never disagreed, no matter if she was personally inconvenienced or not. The animals always came first.

An hour later, she dashed upstairs, chewing the last of her sandwich. Beck would be here any second to retrieve King, and she refused to smell like fish and cat vomit. After gargling with mouthwash, she pulled on a set of aqua scrubs and yanked a brush through her hair.

The overflowing laundry basket mocked her, so she grabbed a double armful and hurried downstairs. Having the family maid, Dora, tend to her clothes was one of the few things she missed from her Philadelphia life.

As she got the washer started, she glanced outside

to the backyard and saw Eric taking King and Pepe on a potty walk. The part-time technician had caught on fast to her procedures and shouldered a lot of the care-taking tasks...for which she was grateful. If her clientele kept expanding, she might manage hiring a full-time tech by next year.

The walkie-talkie on her hip vibrated. "Doctor, your one o'clock appointment has arrived."

She straightened, her heart fluttering. Since she was only a few feet away, she headed down the hallway to reception instead of answering.

Two men stood with erect posture in front of Annie's desk. Almost as if pulled, she took in Beck's appearance first--green T-shirt over khaki shorts. The other man wore a black T-shirt and tan cargo pants.

Annie glanced her way. "There she is."

"Good afternoon, Beck." Danae nodded as she made eye contact...and her stomach tumbled. His crystal blue eyes were just as direct and piercing as she remembered.

"Hello, Danae." Beck stepped forward then swung a hand toward the other man. "I want to introduce Hank Patterson of Brotherhood Protectors."

Her step faltered. The security firm had provided protection when Malin Langstom was stalked after being taken by bank robbers a few months back. Puzzled, she stepped forward and accepted the dark-haired man's extended hand. "Nice to meet you."

"Pleasure's mine, ma'am. Do you have an office

where we could talk?" He glanced around the immediate area.

"You're here with Beck to discuss his dog's condition?" Eyebrow cocked, she glanced at Beck who gave a short nod.

"Of course, in addition to another matter." Hank smiled.

His lips curved but the gesture didn't reach his green eyes. *What is going on here?* "Back here." She led them partway down the hall and turned into her small space. Just this morning, she cleared one of the chairs of patient files and had Annie refile them. She slipped behind her desk and did a double-take when Beck closed the door behind him. Her body tensed. "What's this about?"

"You probably know I run a private security firm here in town." He leaned back and crossed an ankle over the opposite knee.

"I've heard of your company." She looked over to Beck for a clue, but he sat with his body angled in the chair and focused on Hank. "But I don't know what your services have to do with my business."

"My company was hired this morning to, at a minimum, install a security system on your property." Hank waved a hand in an arc. "Including all buildings and the property's perimeter."

"What?" She leaned both forearms on her desk. "Who hired you?"

The men exchanged glances then Hank turned

toward her. "Xenia Orestes, who Beck tells me is your sister."

"She is." Security company services were not cheap. How did Xenia get access to the inheritance they all received when they married or turned twenty-five? Xenia had accomplished neither. "But I really don't understand."

'The break-in, Danae." Beck scooted forward and rested a hand on her desk. "Didn't she warn you last night to be careful?" He shrugged. "Her voice carried."

Looking away from his intense gaze proved impossible. "Yes, but—"

"A security system is another way to keep you safe."

She straightened her spine. Was her lot in life to face down overbearing men? "The break-in was two thousand miles away." She pasted on a smile as she turned toward Hank. "I hardly think I'm at risk here. I really don't want my sister spending her money in this way. Can you refund what she paid?"

"Of course." Hank shook his head. "But I encourage you to reconsider. Two break-ins within six months are unusual." He sat forward. "When Beck and I walked the length of the lot facing the street, we didn't see any cameras."

"Because I don't have any. This place was a family home before I bought it."

"Being outside of town, the lots are oversized, and some involve significant acreage. Who is your closest neighbor? And how far away does that person live?"

At the serious tone of his voice, she swallowed. *This man means business.* "I guess that would be Hiram Hinkle who lives about a mile down the road."

"One point three miles to be exact, and with no line of sight because his farmhouse is surrounded by windbreak trees. The next closest, the Thompson farm, is one point six miles, but a creek runs between the properties. That leaves Gertrude and Philomena Mason at one point nine miles distant. Personally, I wouldn't rely on seventy-year-old widows for much."

"Okay..." Normally, she wouldn't have given those distances a second thought, but she could tell by Hank's manner that he thought they were excessive. She frowned at Beck.

He returned the frown and jerked his head toward Hank.

Clasping her hands in her lap, she listened as the security expert explained the number and positions of the recommended unobtrusive cameras and the simple-to-use computer program for monitoring the activity. "I guess I could use cameras. They might make clients feel better about leaving their pets overnight." She leaned forward. "Did the lack of cameras bother you, Beck, when you had to leave King?"

He cleared his throat. "Frankly, I was too worried about the procedure you described King would endure. But seeing them would have eased my anxiety." He shrugged. "Being ex-military, I put reasonable security measures as a priority."

From what Hank said, the devices were covered by what her sister paid. Why wouldn't she want more security for her business? She could always pay back Xenia. "Sure, they sound like they're needed. Did you want to schedule a date?" For this answer, she looked back at Hank.

He stood and extended a hand. "I'll send out my tech guy this afternoon to do the exterior installations here. Let him know the address, and he can put up ones at your home tomorrow. What's a good time for him to return and load the computer program?"

Wow, so soon. Danae pushed upright. "Uh, either I or my assistant, Eric, are in the office until six, and I assume you guessed I live upstairs."

"Makes the installation easier." He grinned and stepped behind Beck toward the door. "Gotta run. I need to be on a conference call in less than an hour." He nodded toward the seated man. "Beck."

"Thanks, Hank." Beck waved.

Danae sank onto her chair, amazed at the arrangements that were put in place within a fifteen-minute conversation. "The man's a whirlwind."

"He knows the importance of security and how it often comes with a tight timetable." He cocked his head. "I'm glad you agreed to his proposal."

"I'll hash out this matter with my sister later. But I know you're here to be reunited with King." She clasped her hands together on the desktop. "He responded well to the infusion, ate a moderate amount yesterday and this morning, and I wasn't disturbed overnight with any sounds from the kennel."

"Great. I have another matter to discuss."

She eased back, bracing for what he might ask. To date, she'd kept free of romantic entanglements because most of the single men she met were clients. A statement poised on her lips of how she didn't mix her personal and business lives. That rule had been broken last night with their dancing at the Blue Moose. Heat swirled through her core at the memory of being held in his expert hands. She'd even envisioned how they might interact together under the sheets.

"Yeah, I wanted your advice on how to get King re-engaged in scent work."

A professional question? She swallowed hard. That would teach her to daydream.

CHAPTER 4

FOR A MINUTE, Danae's lovely brown eyes unfocused, and Beck swore she'd been remembering them dancing together the night before. More than once today, he'd thought of holding her slim hips between his hands and how her wavy hair tickled his forearms on the dance turns. He flexed his fingers along his thighs to keep from reaching over the desk and hauling her up hard against his body.

"Scent work?"

Her question set him back on track with the problem he'd raised. "He was trained to sniff out explosives and performed that job for four years. But on our last assignment, we came under a brutal attack, intense mortar shelling, and..."

Talking about that horrible day clenched his gut. He hadn't known if he'd crawl out of that battered tank alive. Too often, he awoke in a sweat at the nightmares.

Was he ready to reveal his medical condition? He took a steadying breath. No, the focus was on King. "Since then, he won't perform his usual tasks."

"What have you tried?" She grabbed a pen and a notepad.

"I'm living with another ex-military dog handler, Tag Redmond. We've both run King through a review of his first training exercises and done tons of tennis ball retrieval—both with only fifty-percent success. King and I jog together every day." He spread out his hands. "We have a job pending if he'll get back to his routine. So, I need a new trick."

"What about an agility course?"

"Tag has equipment set up in the back yard he uses for small dogs. But aren't Shepherds too big for those activities?"

"Maybe for competitions. But you want King to find something he enjoys and wants to do." She cocked her head and nibbled on the end of the pen. "Ever heard of lure coursing?"

His breathing hitched. Just a second's glance of a pink tongue but his blood heated. Man, he was developing a major hard-on for this woman. "Uh, no."

"A plastic bag is pulled along the ground on a wire by a pulley system simulating a rabbit hunt. Abrupt turns have to be made, and most dogs love it. Although, the participants are usually sight hounds. If you could get King interested in chasing something, then the next step is to add scent along the chase path." She tapped her pen on the desktop. "Finally, you switch him over to following a scent alone."

He'd seen how her eyes lit up as she described the activity. "You've run a dog in this sport before."

"Years ago and back east." As she swiveled the chair from side to side, she smiled. "The family had a couple of Pharaoh Hounds, and my brother, Aleksy, and I competed in a youth division."

"What about around here?" Providing a whole new type of distraction might work. He scooted his chair closer, wishing the desk didn't create such a barrier. "Can you think of a place to take him today?" The sooner he and King both had an actual job—not just hanging at Tag's place—the better.

"Today? Hmm." She bit her lip and glanced up at the ceiling.

Beck admired her tanned, slender neck that led down to—

"Oh, I know." A smile flashed. "A rancher between here and Bozeman has a course set up by his barn." She jiggled the computer mouse to refresh the screen. "Let me look up his info, and I'll put you in touch with him."

The idea of being passed off didn't sit right. Spending time with her was what he wanted. He ran a hand over his face. *Keep things together.* "What about coming along? I'd be grateful for any expert tips you have."

The moment she looked away, he sensed her hesitation. Something told him if he didn't get her to agree that she'd erect a wall to keep him out. And that was definitely not where he wanted to be. "What's your schedule like?"

"Releasing King is my last required duty of the afternoon." She glanced back in his direction. "So, I'm free until performing the night rounds which don't happen until seven or so."

About five hours. In that time, he could learn a lot about this woman who had already worked her way under his skin. "Give me the drive time plus an hour." He'd figure out later how to cajole more time together. "I'll know by then if King enjoys it enough for me to research more about this sport."

Her eyes lit. "I went out to a competition on a mobile call shortly after I moved here. Poor Whippet sprained an ankle. I ended up staying for the remainder of the runs." She braced both palms on the desktop. "I'd love to see if King takes to the sport."

"Great. Now, I'm anxious to see King's recovery for myself." He stood and followed her to the back of the house, through a mud room, and onto a back porch. About sixty feet away stood a long structure surrounded by chain-link fencing.

As they moved across the yard, he did his best not to stare at her ass jiggling just a little under her cotton, loose-fitting pants. He remembered what her figure looked like cinched into the sexy, low slung jeans. How the soft denim hugged her curves and outlined her slim legs.

Danae swung open a door into a small room with cupboards, a counter, and a sink.

Must be where food is prepared. Everything looked neat and clean. From the other side of the nearby door came a few barks, mostly high-pitched ones.

"Here's the collar he wore when he arrived." She retrieved it from a cupboard. "Did you bring his leash?"

Damn. "Left it in the car. No problem, though. King'll stick by my side with just voice commands." He collected the leather strap, brushing his fingers over her hand.

Her eyes widened. "Well…" She nibbled her lower lip. "Since no other appointments are scheduled, I guess him going with you off-leash will be all right." Danae opened the door, exposing a double row of kennel spaces, and swept a hand toward the concrete aisle running between them. "He's in pen four. Get reacquainted. I'll meet you in front in about ten minutes. I need to give Eric final instructions and tell him about the computer tech."

Beck stepped forward, brushing against her in his haste. He registered her gasp, but he was intent on getting to his dog.

King stood with his nose pressed through the gate's metal square, his entire rear end swaying with the ferocity of his wagging tail.

"*God hund.*" Beck lifted the pin latch and dropped to one knee inside. A quick appraisal of King's face showed his lip was back to its normal size. Not that he hadn't believed Danae's assessment, but confirmation of the facts was a Ranger habit. This dog and he had been through a lot. Relief that his buddy was no longer under stress produced a chuckle. "Hey, King. Feeling okay?" He shoved his fingers deep into the dog's fur behind his ears and scratched, probably needing to reconnect as much as the dog did. "You sure look and sound better, boy."

King lowered his head and pressed against Beck's chest.

After buckling on the collar, he led the dog from the kennel. Then he ran King through a series of stops and starts around the interior of the fenced yard before stopping near the back porch. Just to re-establish the dominance order. "*Sitta*, King." Out of the corner of his eye, he watched to make sure King obeyed before releasing him. "*Fri*."

King sniffed an erratic path over the patchy grass then moved to the fence and lifted a leg against a post.

Letting the dog wander, Beck grabbed his phone and did a quick read on the sport of lure coursing so he'd know what to expect. The dogs in the videos were definitely thinner, but Danae was right. They looked like they were having a great time, and the whole point was to get King interested. He pocketed the phone. "*Komma*."

Head erect, King bounded close, circling to Beck's left side.

"*Söka*." Beck waited until King slipped between his

legs. Knees bent, he then worked the dog in tight formation through a series of turns. Arms held in front of his chest, he pantomimed holding a level rifle and guided King, positioned between his legs, with alternating voice commands and knee taps.

By the time they were ten feet from the truck, he realized they performed for an audience of one. To show off, he executed an about face, changed direction to circle around the back of his truck, and stopped at the passenger door. "*Stanna.*" He eased upward from the armed stance and ruffled King's ears. "*Ned.*"

King lowered to the ground and laid his chin between his paws.

Beck silently counted to three to make sure King held his position before glancing toward the porch. "You ready?" He spotted her nod and watched her loose strides as she approached. A lemon-yellow sleeveless top covered her torso and a pair of tight jeans clung to her hips and legs. Athletic shoes completed the outfit, which were probably more practical than cowboy boots. But he really liked the cowgirl image she had going last night.

"Is that German you're speaking?" She stopped next to the truck door.

A clean scent like basil mixed with orange wafted his way. "Nah, Swedish. Lots of handlers train with German, but by using a different language, I know King will respond to just me." He shrugged as he opened the door and cupped her elbow to help her climb up. "Besides, I grew up around older relatives who are native speakers." Talking about his upbringing always made him want to check his six to see who listened. Enough crazies lived in this world who didn't agree with American military policies abroad.

"I know what that situation's like, only my relatives speak Greek." She laughed. "Literally."

Orestes. Yeah, he should have guessed her nationality. One of his buddies on the team had been Christofides, and Beck heard a similar lilt on certain pronunciations between the two people.

"King, *komma*." Beck trotted around the back of the truck and signaled for King to jump into the seat. He ran his hand along the crease of the seat. When his fingertips brushed her hip, he glanced up and shrugged. "Sorry, searching for the restraining strap."

She scooted toward the door. "Don't worry."

"Can you hand me that harness at your feet? I should have put this on while we were outside." *But I was too busy focusing on you, pretty lady*.

Danae leaned over then straightened and held out the protective gear. "Glad to see you take safety precautions for your pet."

"That's me, Mr. Precaution. Might have taken some shit about double and triple checking gear and plans, but I survived a decade in the Rangers." He settled the canvas and Kevlar vest over King's back then nudged his front legs in succession to signal him to lift a paw. After clipping the buckles into place, he snapped the end of the restraining strap to the D-ring on the top loop. "We're headed toward Bozeman, right?"

"Yes, the ranch is only about fifteen miles away." The breeze blew in the window and lifted her hair in a long wave.

Beck gripped the steering wheel to stop himself from reaching to touch it again. What he wanted was to wind his fingers in the length of her strands and slowly reel her close for a languid kiss. By the time he pulled onto the highway heading south, he saw King shifted so his head rested on Danae's thigh.

As she looked at the passing scenery, she ran long fingers through King's ruff.

Beck couldn't keep his gaze away, wishing he was the recipient of her gentle touch. He had to get his mind onto something else. "How long have you lived in Eagle Rock?"

"A little over six months." She turned to look his way. "And you?"

"Two." The air blowing through the truck cab was warm but not enough to need the air conditioner. Because of the places he'd been stationed, he was used to warm air on his skin.

Several minutes passed while they figured out which of the townspeople they both knew. Then they commiserated on the need to drive to Bozeman or Livingston for groceries or entertainment like bowling or seeing a movie.

"I've started ordering food online for home delivery." She grabbed a fistful of her hair and held it close to her neck with one hand. "So much easier. Especially when I've worked a ten- or eleven-hour day."

A schedule he knew well but until now, he hadn't realized those hours could be a veterinarian's fate. "That happen often?"

"Often enough to make sure my kitchen cupboards are well-stocked."

"What about fruits and vegetables?" Wonder if Tag knew about this alternative? He marveled at how easily conversation flowed with her, the rapport not one he'd experienced with many women.

"I can get those items delivered, too." She jabbed her arm over King's back. "Turn left here."

Beck braked, screeched the tires, and turned onto a gravel road marked with an arched sign proclaiming Circle P Ranch. He shot her a narrowed glance over his shoulder before focusing on the rutted road running between rail fencing.

"Don't give me that glare. I've only been here once before." She braced a hand on the dashboard. "Larry said he'd be in the south field, but he'd watch for us."

Beck surveyed the green alfalfa field to his left. Over the two-foot-tall plants rose a dust trail. "Looks like we've been spotted."

Ten minutes later, with introductions handled, Larry Pelletier scratched the layout of the course in the dirt beside the corral.

"What command do you use?" Beck glanced down at a leashed King sitting at attention on his left side.

The thirty-something man's dark eyebrows rose. "Commands? A dog's natural instinct is to chase prey, and that's what they see as the bags on the wire shoot away. You just start the motor then release your grip on the collar."

Beck refrained from arguing, because Larry couldn't know that King's specialized training kept him in place until he heard a command. Except for breaking protocol to chase a rabbit. "Got it. Should we stand anyplace special?"

Danae tapped his arm. "I'll show you." She headed away from the corral.

"*Komma*." Beck strode to follow, running over in his mind which command from those King knew was most appropriate.

"Here." She pointed. "See the white blobs in that direction? Those are the bags that will be in motion throughout the course."

He tracked the wire for as far as he could before it disappeared in the low weeds. "I see them." He knelt at King's side, gripped the dog collar, and unclipped the lead. "Go ahead and signal Larry."

Danae stood and waved a hand over her head.

A whirring sounded.

Beck tensed, hoping this idea worked. When the first bag moved, he released his grip. "King, *fri*."

The dog jumped forward a foot or so then stopped and glanced over his shoulder.

Danae took off running along the wire, long hair streaming behind her. "Come on, King. Let's go."

Beck snapped a flattened hand, fingers pointing forward. "*Gå, gå*, King."

King leaped after her and, within a few strides, outpaced her. By the time the moving bag made a ninety-degree turn, he was running at top speed.

About twenty feet away, Danae stopped and shaded her eyes with a raised hand, pumping her other hand in the air. "Run, King. Run!"

Watching his buddy race for the quarry brought a lump to Beck's throat. From what he could see of King's expression, the dog was into the chase. The first hurdle to his recovery had been crossed. All because of one beautiful woman. Beck jogged to where she stood, scooped her into a bear hug, and spun them around. "Thank you, Doctor Danae."

Squealing, she braced her hands on his shoulders. "He's loving it, isn't he? And you're welcome." Looking down, she grinned from within a dark curtain of wavy hair.

Her belly pressed against his chest and, at eye level, her breasts tantalized. But what captured him was the glimmer in her dark eyes. The air heated, as if a sirocco appeared out of nowhere and surrounded them. He loosened his hold and inched her downward until they were nose to nose, her feet still several inches off the ground. Then he leaned forward and grazed his lips across hers, hoping like hell he wasn't overstepping any boundaries. Holding his breath, he eased back and waited, watching her relaxed expression.

Her eyelids fluttered open. "That's it?"

Oh, hell no. Cupping a hand on the back of her head, he pressed her close before settling his lips over hers for a long, wet, exploratory kiss.

A moan vibrated her mouth. She wrapped her legs around his waist and rocked forward, brushing the tips of her breasts across his chest.

Beck pressed back, savoring the drag of tight points against his skin through his T-shirt. Blood pumped into his groin, making him rock hard. The sensuality he glimpsed while they danced bloomed, and she writhed in his arms. Their mouths fused and their bodies strained closer. He slid his hand from her head to support her shapely butt and rubbed her crotch over his jeans fly. The pressure intensified, swirling desire though his body.

Beats of loud pounding sounded in the air.

Their hearts? Blood in his good ear?

No, the rhythm of four paws hitting the ground. Beck realized where they stood. He drew back and rested his forehead against hers. "Ah, pretty lady. We're pretty much on display here."

King skidded to a stop, panting.

"Oh, yeah." She unlocked her ankles and grabbed his shoulders to slip her legs down his sides until she stood on her own. Without looking at him, she dropped to her knees and ruffled King's ears. "You liked that chase, didn't you, boy?"

Beck ran a hand thorough his hair, fighting against being obvious about catching his breath.

Larry whistled.

Grateful the moment's rest allowed his erection to soften, Beck turned in the rancher's direction.

"Ready for another go?"

What the hell? Scowling, Beck clenched his fists and stepped forward.

Shaking his head, Larry waved outstretched hands. "For the dog, I mean."

"Yeah." He turned and connected with Danae's gaze. "You got him?"

Nodding, she gripped King's collar and walked him around until he faced the course. "Tell me what you said before."

"*Fri* means he's free or released from training."

"No, the other one."

"*Gå* means go." A thrill shot through him that she wanted to communicate with his dog in his practiced way.

She mouthed the two-syllable word then waved toward Larry.

The machine whirred, and the wire snapped tight an instant before the bags shot away.

"*Gå, gå, gå.*" Danae jumped to her feet.

King lit out, running full throttle.

Beck hooked his thumbs through his front belt loops to keep from reaching for her again. This time, he wanted to watch King run the whole course.

As a heavier dog, the Shepherd struggled to scramble and change directions after the sudden turns, but his gaze stayed focused on the target. This time, when King rejoined them, he flopped onto his belly and panted with loud rasps.

"*God hund.*" Beck dropped to one knee and scratched under his chin. "*Du sprang så fort.*" He glanced up into her inquisitive gaze. "I told him he was a good dog and he ran so fast." He reached to his back pocket and pulled out the leather lead then snapped it on King's collar. "We should let Larry get back to his work." As they said their goodbyes, Beck received the gracious offer to use the rancher's equipment again.

As he drove the rutted road, Beck rolled over in his mind the best ways to extend the outing. The dash clock read three-thirty--probably too early for a meal. Maybe he could ask about the equipment and where to buy it.

"I'm starved. What about you?"

"Really?" He glanced to the side. "I thought now was too early."

"Not when a client shifted her appointment and all I ate for lunch was half a sandwich."

"Sounds great, but where should we go?"

"Where else but Al's Diner?" She giggled. "I'll call

ahead so the food will be ready, and we can take it back to my house." She looked at him then glanced away.

"Fine by me. Cheeseburger, fries, and a vanilla shake. And order two plain burger patties for King, no salt. He earned them."

"Good." She bent over to retrieve her phone.

Fifteen minutes later, he handed the sacks through the passenger door. "You'll have to keep them on the floor between your feet or risk being mauled. King loses his manners around beef."

She grinned and nodded before leaning over.

When he climbed into the cab, he spotted two wide-eyed faces turned his way. He sniffed the air then lowered his head close to King. "Did you just feed him a French fry?"

She blinked fast then shrugged. "Just one won't hurt him. I am his doctor."

Beck laughed as he steered toward the road leading out of town. When was the last time he felt this carefree? The houses grew farther apart as they continued south. The two events that made him happy warred for supremacy—spending time with Danae or glimpsing King's former spirit. Glancing at the sunlight creeping toward the mountain ridge, he pondered on their relative importance.

"Hey, what's wrong with my car?" Danae lurched forward to point out the windshield. "Look."

Her silver SUV listed to one side on flattened tires. Beck parked in front of the vet office, cut the engine, and extended his right arm to grasp her shoulder. "Stay here." After a perusal of the roofline to check for the security cameras, he slid out of the truck and bent to retrieve the knife he kept in a sheath under the driver's seat. Old habits died hard.

Walking in a flexed knee position, he made a wide circle around the rear of the vehicle, knife held along one thigh, until he saw no one crouched in hiding. He dropped to a push-up position to check under the car then jumped to his feet.

Holding out a flattened hand to keep her in the truck, he jogged to the porch and glanced in the front room window as he tried the door. Locked. Nothing inside looked out of place. Both were good. He tucked the knife in his belt and returned to the passenger side.

Danae jumped out and stomped over to her car. "Look what someone did." She squatted and ran her fingers over the tires. "The sidewall is slashed." She moved to the rear tire. "Same here."

Beck released King from the safety strap and fastened on the leash. Not that he thought the dog would snap into action, but King might as well be visible in case anyone watched from a distance. He'd already scanned the immediate area and hadn't spotted any vehicles. But someone could be hiding among bushes along the road or in a neighboring field.

"Oh no."

He spun at the shock in her voice and ran to where she stood staring at a scrap of paper. "Let me see."

A shaky hand extended the note.

He read, "Give up what you took, Mrs. Charonopoulos, and this ends." His gut clenched. The lowlife knew the correct car to vandalize. Again, he scanned the note, and his breath hitched. *Danae is married?*

CHAPTER 5

DANAE WATCHED the emotions flash across Beck's face-
-from concerned to confused to astonished. Her
stomach churned. What must he think of her?

"You're married?" Eyebrows arched high, he took a
step back.

He probably wasn't even aware he'd moved away
like she'd suddenly contracted a contagious disease.
"Divorced." Who disliked her enough to wreck her
tires? Pulse racing, she dug into her purse for her keys.
The note carried her married name, meaning whatever
was going on somehow related to her ex-husband.

Giles.

Admittedly, the man was infuriating enough to rile
anyone to act irrationally. But why was she being
targeted? First, her bedroom back home in Philadelphia, and now, this vandalism. Plus the phone call
yesterday that no longer seemed like a crank one.

Hurrying into the building, she checked the receptionist desk then her office for signs of a break-in. Seeing nothing out of place, she called Eric, pacing to the back door as she listened to the phone ring. A twist of the knob verified it remained locked.

"Hey, boss. If you're calling because I cut out early, I can explain."

"No, Eric. I told you to leave when you were finished." Actually, she didn't even know what time it was now but that detail wasn't important. "Was the security program installed on the computer? If so, how do I access it?" She turned and spotted Beck at the receptionist desk, his hand hovering over the keyboard.

"I left the paperwork on your desk."

She slipped into her office but didn't see anything that she didn't recognize. "Hmm."

"Is something wrong? Do you need me to come back?"

Guilt flashed through her thoughts. Did she really need to get her assistant involved? She could handle this issue. "I'll be fine. Enjoy your evening." Then she punched End on the call. In the third drawer she opened, she found the paperwork he'd left. Why didn't he say he put it in a drawer?

With the single sheet in hand, she walked back to the main office. "Here's the information on the security program."

"I've accessed it, but the program's not registered.

Just need you to set up a user name and create a pass-word." He stood and moved aside.

Danae slipped into the chair and poised her fingers over the keyboard. Then she set them into her lap. "Would you mind moving to the other side of the counter?" She glanced over her shoulder. "Sorry, trust is a major issue since my divorce. And I've only known—"

"Say no more." Beck walked to the counter and leaned his forearms on the surface.

She completed the requirements to register the program and then clicked over to her cloud storage account and added the password to her spreadsheet. Not the most-protected system available, but she didn't have top-secret data connected to her business.

A glance at the paperwork didn't provide instructions on how to open the program. Great, one of those intuitive methods that she was horrible at. The main reason she'd hired a receptionist who was more computer savvy was so she could spend more time on tending living creatures.

A quick scan of the screen didn't point to the next step or button to click. Squinting, she pursed her lips. The Internet, email, and the accounting program were about all she used. "I've registered it. Do you know what comes next?" For this operation, she was willing to let him mess around to get the system started so she vacated the chair.

Shaking his head, he pointed toward the screen.

"Probably straight forward. Just click on the company's icon on the desktop and then enter your password."

As soon as she did as he said, the screen displayed a black-and-gray image split into six sections. She scanned the images. "Okay, I see your truck and my SUV and shots of the back yard."

Beck stepped to her left side and leaned a hand on the desk. "Do you see any archived files?" He pointed at the left sidebar. "Click there."

She did and saw a folder labeled with the current date, but it only contained the images she saw.

"That doesn't seem right. The program should have been recording from the moment it was connected." He picked up the security company's form. "Here...type in this URL and security code to download the earlier recording." He straightened and reached for his cell phone. "We need to report this incident to the sheriff."

Again, his take-charge attitude grated. Why did he think he was the one to make the call? She stood and braced her hands on the desk. Her phone was in her purse where she'd dumped it on her office desk. But that fact shouldn't matter. She could handle her own damn problems. "Beck, I'll make the call. The damage was done to *my* car in front of *my* office on *my* property."

He stilled, finger poised above the phone screen, and shot her a sideways glance. His posture relaxed. "Of course, you should. Let me download the earlier footage and look for any clues to the vandal's ID then

I'll get the food out of the truck." He slipped into the chair and started typing, focus directed toward the monitor. "If you're busy when I get back with the food, where's your kitchen?"

Reality hit. She'd invited him to eat here, so she'd be letting someone upstairs into her personal space. Danae jerked her head. "Up the stairs at the end of the hallway then head toward the back of the house. It's on your left."

An hour later, the sheriff had come, shot photos of the tire damage, interviewed them both, and headed back to the station. He didn't hold out much hope of locating any suspects but, at least, a report would be on file.

Danae stood in front of the small microwave in her kitchen, waiting for her food to reheat. The fries would be limp, but they'd be calories. Beck looked so wrong sitting in one of the mismatched wooden chairs at her round table topped with a strawberry vine tablecloth. His size dwarfed the furnishings.

"Do you delay meals often?" He shifted the ketchup bottle from hand to hand then set it down.

"I kept thinking Sheriff Barron would arrive any second. I didn't want to be eating when he came."

"Why? Joe knew he arrived near supper time, and people have to eat." A muscled shoulder shrugged. "He didn't mind me eating during the interview."

The manners instilled by her mother might not fit every situation, but Danae couldn't deny they were part of her social habits. A bell dinged. *Saved.* She pulled out the plate with her burger and moved to the table, claiming a chair opposite him. "Do you want a drink or something else?" She hated to be the only one eating. "Maybe some fruit?"

"Not yet." He patted his flat stomach. "I wouldn't turn down a beer, though."

"Don't have any." She unwrapped the soggy paper from the burger and rubbed greasy fingers together. "I think I have an open bottle of white wine." She scooted back her chair.

He grimaced then smoothed his expression. "Stop, Danae. Eat your food and quit worrying about me."

The first bite of the burger tasted heavenly, with a mix of grilled onions and rich meat. With the second and third, she noticed the limp lettuce and the watery tomatoes. But she kept taking bites.

Beck clasped his hands on the table top, his body still.

She glanced up from readying for her next bite and caught his gaze. "What?'

"Just waiting for you to finish."

"Then can you go over to the other room and turn on the TV? I don't need an observer."

A grin flashed. "Ah, the lady gets grouchy when she hasn't eaten." He shoved to a stand and sauntered across the hall to her living room.

King scrambled up from where he'd laid on the rag rug in front of the sink and trotted behind.

The minute he disappeared, she regretted speaking in such a harsh tone. Being snappy wasn't part of her personality, but the man had such a masculine presence that he made her nervous.

Cheers from a sports event of some type floated through the open doorway.

The sounds were odd within her home. Since moving here, she'd had complete control of what shows to watch and athletic events were no longer part of her selections. Two bites later, she carried her plate and soda into the living room and sat at the opposite end of the couch.

Beck glanced over at her plate then turned back toward the set.

The screen displayed a baseball game in progress and, by the excited voice of the announcer, the score must be close. She bit into a soggy French fry then set down the plate on the middle cushion. Maybe if she'd reheated them in the oven, they wouldn't be mush.

"That's all you're eating?" His eyebrow rose.

"Want them?" she waved a hand at the remaining food. "I'll warn you…they taste horrible."

"Nope." He clicked off the television and angled a leg so he faced her head on. "We need to discuss how this afternoon's incident changes your security."

"Security?" She wrinkled her brow. "The cameras are in place, and I know how to access the program. What else has to change?"

"Protocol, as set out by Brotherhood Protectors,

states the subject needs to be moved to an alternate location following a physical threat."

Moved? He had to be kidding. Didn't the man realize what her job entailed? Danae squinted, studying his face. "You're making that up." Damn, she wouldn't want to play poker against this guy.

"Am not."

"Well, I'm not leaving." She crossed her arms over her chest then immediately dropped them, not wanting to appear too defiant. Certainly, they could come to a compromise. Like jamming chairs under doorknobs and putting dowels in window tracks. She stiffened. Did he think someone might break into her house? "I have animals to protect."

"Figured you'd say that." He stood and ran his hands down the front of his pants. "Then, we're driving to my place so I can pack what I'll need and pick up King's food."

Gawking, she stared upward. Her seated position on the refurbished couch put her at a disadvantage. "You're not serious."

"Your sister paid Hank to keep you safe, and that protection just changed to second-tier service."

Danae knew she wouldn't like what he inferred and mentally braced herself. "Which is?"

"A twenty-four/seven bodyguard detail." He jabbed a thumb into his chest. "Me, shadowing your every move."

Crap. She sucked in a breath. She hadn't yet

processed the amazing kiss they'd shared this after-noon. And now she'd have no privacy? This man who'd sparked her libido to life like no one else had would be living under her roof? "Is that step really necessary?"

Beck widened his stance and crossed his arms. "Do you want someone entering the kennel and hurting those animals? Or worse, breaking into the house? How are you prepared to combat those events?"

She jumped up, jammed her hands on her hips, and glared. "Don't use scare tactics. Just help me make this place more secure."

"Damn, you're sexy when your eyes flash." A muscle in his jaw clenched.

Changing the topic was what her ex did when he wanted his way. Huffing out a breath, she turned to reach toward her plate. "Don't distract me." Hands braced on her hips applied gentle push-pull pressure until she turned. Then he pulled her flush against his hard body. She braced both hands on his biceps, and her pulse raced.

"I'm not the one being distracting." His gaze centered on her lips.

Her breath hitched, drawing in Beck's scent of burgers and onions with a hint of faded cologne. The focus in his blue eyes held her immobile. When was the last time a man looked at her like she was his favorite meal? Way too long. Her mouth dried, and she licked her lips.

"Not helping."

Before she could process what he'd said, she felt his hand cup her chin and angle her head. Then sensations swept through her body --his lips pressed hard against hers, tongue slipped between her lips, her breasts flattened against his rock-hard chest, a thigh shoved between her legs. Her body responded. She slid her hands up his arms and grabbed his shoulders. Their bodies strained together from knee to chest, but she wanted more. Rolling onto her toes, she skimmed her right hand up his neck and toyed with the strands of hair at his nape.

With a groan, Beck set her away from his body and released his hold. He cleared his throat and lifted a hand toward his left ear then ran it over the top of his head. "We'd better get going. You need to carry out the night tasks around seven, right?"

Swaying, Danae blinked and fought to catch her breath. What just happened? Had she done something wrong?

CHAPTER 6

THE NEXT MORNING, Danae slapped down the blaring alarm without opening her eyes and nestled into the cocoon of bedsheets and light quilt.

A sound that shouldn't be present in her normally quiet house kept her from drifting off again. Water ran in the downstairs bathroom. Her houseguest. Beck must be showering. She really should get up.

Smiling, she squirmed deeper into the mattress and pictured his large frame in that outdated, half-sized shower stall. Broad, soapy hands rubbing over ridged abdominals and tight pectorals. Sluicing water carving sudsy trails across brawny shoulders, along tight ribs, and down bulging quads. A warm hand circling her taut breast, ready to respond to the slightest touch, and caressing a path over her slick stomach then diving into the nest of dark curls between her thighs.

Her pussy quivered, and need swirled low in her

belly. Imagining his hands on her skin drove her blood pressure into the danger zone. Those two words sparked, and lyrics from long ago ran unbidden through her mind. Humming, she ran her hands over her body, scraping the cotton nightshirt across her breasts tightening her nipples into hard points. Highway to the Danger Zone.

Now, she couldn't get the damn Kenny Loggins tune out of her head. Then she dipped her hand under the covers and beneath her T-shirt to rub her clit. Her fingers came away slickened with dewy liquid. After another couple of circles, she arched her back, moving her hand faster and in tighter circles until the pressure built to a quivering release. Waves of sensation and flutters of tingles pulsed in her sex. Dropping back to the mattress, she kept her knees crooked and let out a low moan as the delightful spasms eased.

Two knocks tapped her bedroom door. "You all right in there?"

Her body tensed, chasing away the last of her orgasm. She sighed. "I'm just fine." Her voice sounded strangled even to her own ears.

"You sure? Thought I heard a satisfied moan."

"Go away, Beck."

"What should I wear on my first day as your new intern?"

Oh, crap. Was he standing outside her door in just a bath towel slung low on his hips? With water droplets dotting his chest and maybe a rivulet running between his pecs? Would his skin be smooth or covered in a light coating of hair?

"Danae?"

This time, she jackknifed into a sitting position and opened her eyes to hopefully prevent any more daydreams. "Scrubs. One of Eric's sets should be downstairs in the walk-in closet across the hall from the bathroom."

"He's the guy I saw the first day I brought in King?"

"That's him."

"His clothes won't fit me."

"You need to look like you're an intern." She dangled her legs over the side of the bed. Talking through a closed door was strange, but she didn't think she could handle seeing him in her still-aroused and aware state. "Scrubs are loose-fitting, and I think his are a medium-large combo."

"Sweetheart, I'm not a medium anything."

I so did not need that image. She flounced back on the mattress, arms extended. How would she get through her first sight of him, let alone an entire day?

"I hope those damn things come in a color other than pastel." His footsteps padded down the hallway toward the stairs, echoed by the tick-tick of doggie toenails.

She grabbed a clean set of pale yellow scrubs from her dresser drawer, along with panties and a bra, and stepped into her bathroom. Maybe a pulsating showerhead could pound some sense into her, and she'd stop drooling over the man. Two dynamite kisses should not have turned her into a starry-eyed fool.

With the air in the bathroom still steamy, she leaned toward the fogged mirror and tilted her head to brush on a single coat of mascara. Three quick swipes on each side. An almost-invisible accent and a smear of tinted lip balm. Very understated but the makeup did make her look a bit more rested.

Bending over, she brushed a pick through her wavy hair to remove the tangles and grabbed the bulk with one fist at the crown of her head. Off her wrist, she pulled a scrunchie, ready to secure the mass into a messy bun. Or maybe not.

Moments later, she emerged and turned left toward the kitchen for her usual green tea and whole wheat toast with almond butter. The scents that rolled down the hallway made her stomach rumble. Robust coffee and pan-fried potatoes with onions and peppers. She walked into the kitchen and clapped a hand over her mouth to keep in a laugh.

The fabric of the scrubs' top strained across his shoulder blades so tight it looked ready to split any second. The hem of the pant legs hit him mid-ankle-- which actually was the new pant length. But she wouldn't say a word. "Morning. Everything smells great." She moved to the cupboard to grab plates but stopped when she spotted them next to the stove.

He glanced over his shoulder, eyebrows raised. "I couldn't find any eggs, and I don't know about this vegetable sausage. But it was the only thing I could find in your freezer that resembled meat. Didn't you eat a burger yesterday?"

She moved to the coffeemaker that she almost never used for only one person. "I supply the cook at Al's with a box of pseudo-beef patties to use when I order burgers. When I'm home, I eat plant-based food." She poured half a cup and lifted it to her nose to inhale the rich scent.

"Oh." He crimped his mouth tight and turned back to the stove.

"You really didn't have to cook all this." Although her mouth watered just looking at the food. "I usually grab something on the run for breakfast."

"That's why you're too skinny." He leaned down to watch as he adjusted the propane flame. "I know you're not happy with this arrangement. So I figured I'd make myself useful."He grabbed a plate, served a heaping spoonful of potatoes and two sausage patties then held it out.

Her eyes rounded. "I can't eat all that."

"Try."

"Thanks." She took the plate and walked to the table. The first bite of potatoes tasted so good she closed her eyes in ecstasy. She often struggled to make the most basic recipe.

A moment later, he set his plate and went back to pour a cup of coffee. When he returned, he lowered slowly into the chair then popped back up.

"Forget something?" She munched on a wedge of sausage, wondering if the patty tasted better because someone else cooked it.

"Nope." He lifted his plate and started eating standing up. "Don't you know about the new fitness craze where you're supposed to spend more of your time on your feet?"

Steam wafted across her cheeks as she looked at him over her coffee mug. "I thought that was for desk work."

"I can't sit." He set down his plate again then lifted the front of the cotton shirt. "The damn pants are too small and pinch my..." Redness invaded his cheeks.

At the sight of those bulging abdominals she'd wondered about, she swallowed hard. To keep from dropping her jaw, she bit the inside of her cheek. Cut marks arrowed over his hips and disappeared below the drawstring waistband that hung three inches below his tight navel. Her blood thumped in her ears. Lifting her chin, she met his gaze and tilted her head. "Guess you were right about the size."

"If I sit, I feel like..." He looked away then his gaze snapped back. "Hell, you're a doctor. The crotch pinches my balls and strangles me." He released the shirt and grabbed his plate again.

She fought from sighing at the cotton barrier now hiding his taut and tanned skin. Focusing on her plate, she consoled herself with learning his chest was covered with a sparse layer of light brown hair. Now, she knew exactly what to picture. She had to stop thinking about his body. "Did you sleep well?" Great, that question produced an image of him in her guest room, filling the space of the full-sized bed.

"Almost always do. Still getting used to longer sleep sessions, instead of catching fifteen or thirty minutes here or there."

"Sounds awful. I need at least six hours of solid sleep, or I'm a wreck."

"Then you must have achieved that. Cuz from where I'm standing, you look nothing like a wreck." He walked over to the sink and set his plate inside then braced both hands on the counter. The shirt strained like a second skin across his chest. "I like your hair down."

Heat flushed her cheeks. *He noticed.* Only with great restraint did she keep from lifting a hand to rearrange the strands over her shoulder. Most of it was contained by a clip, but she'd left the lower section loose. Danae walked her dishes to the sink. Beck stood only a few inches away and the clean scent of his soap filled her senses.

She wished she had the right to ask what caused him to pull back last night, right when the kiss had revived her hibernating libido. But he was under her roof to do a job, not to end her sexual dry spell. Although she imagined he could fulfill that task exceedingly well. *Stop the fantasies.* Think of a neutral topic. "Should we inform Annie and Eric about why you're here?"

"Don't you think that's only fair?"

"Of course, you're right." She looked up at him and connected with his intense gaze. The baby blue of the shirt made his eyes pop. Hearing that fact would probably make him want to strip. Not a bad idea... She sucked in a shaky breath and summoned a smile. "Let's get this day started."

Downstairs, she headed straight for the desk and murmured words to the injured bird before bringing the computer from sleep mode.

King settled at her feet.

"I already checked last night's footage." Beck leaned both forearms on the counter. "No humans activated the cameras after we walked the animals last night. Saw a pair of coyotes along the back perimeter and a couple of raccoons knocked over the trash can. You need a heavier one."

She shrugged. "I know I do, but I figure the animals must be hungry."

"You're too soft-hearted." He grinned. "Tell me what I'll be doing as an intern-slash-secret bodyguard."

Her mind had been too preoccupied with the fact he was here all the time that she hadn't thought about the ruse. "Mostly grunt work. Wiping down the exam tables after each visit, cleaning up messes, being an extra pair of hands if I need an animal restrained."

"Not like the Great Dane incident, I hope."

She laughed. "You'd be preventing something like that."

The door opened. "Morning, boss. Oh." Annie stood at the front door with her mouth agape. Her gaze ran up and down Beck's back.

"Morning, Annie." Danae glared at her employee until she shut the door. "You remember Beck with the German Shepherd we treated a few days ago?"

"Hey, lady doc. Whose truck is parked out front?" Eric sauntered down the hallway from the back entrance.

"Good, you're both here." Danae stood and waved a hand. "Beck here is more than a new client. As of last night, he's been assigned to provide security for the premises."

"What?" Annie frowned and shot Eric a look.

"You need more than the cameras provide?" Eric narrowed his gaze and studied Beck.

"I work for Brotherhood Protectors, which I'm sure you've heard about. Concern has arisen about Danae being the target of a possible stalker. Yesterday afternoon, when the office was vacant, two of her tires were slashed."

Annie glanced between the two with a narrowed gaze. "Her SUV looked fine when I parked just now."

"They were replaced early this morning. I checked the footage myself and recognized a BP employee." He met her gaze with an upraised eyebrow.

Wow, Hank's company provides great service. Danae

nodded and scooted to the left side of the desk to let him have the chair.

"And she's had at least one threatening phone call. I'll expect both of you to report anything out of the ordinary. " Beck braced a hand on the desk and leaned over the back of the computer chair. "Let me demonstrate how to access the security feed from the motion-activated cameras."

As Beck gave instructions, Danae saw a sliver of tanned skin at his hip where the shirt had ridden up. The sight reminded her of seeing his torso earlier, and her heart rate sped. Shaking away that image, she focused on his precise instructions and how he made sure both employees could manipulate the features of the program. In his past, he must have been in a command position. So much about him she didn't know.

When he turned to look over his right shoulder, she spotted a small device at the back of his left ear. A hearing aid? Was that the reason he pulled away last night? She remembered his explanation for why King stopped his detection work. Had Beck been injured, as well?

"As you can see, I'm posing as an intern." Beck straightened and jerked his head in her direction. "Doing so lets me shadow Danae without raising too much suspicion."

"You both are expected to treat him like he's a part of the staff. We'll figure out the tasks as we go along, but obviously, he can't do anything that needs specific skills." She glanced between the two and got the reactions she expected—Eric shrugged and Annie flashed a flirty grin. "Who are we seeing today?" With a jolt, she realized she hadn't reviewed the daily schedule because of their lure course outing yesterday. That oversight was a first.

With the day's schedule in hand, she led Beck through the cat exam room to the procedure room. "This space is the hub of our activities. When we have to perform a procedure that might make the owner uncomfortable, we bring the animal here." She patted the metal exam table. On one end was an adjustable metal post with a sturdy D-ring at the top.

An hour and three patients later, Danae discovered no matter where Beck stood in the small exam rooms, she was too focused on his presence. Worse were the mental images she'd had upon first awakening were never far from her thoughts, making her skin zing with awareness. She had no idea how long she could keep up the pretense.

BECK STEPPED FORWARD and held the Beagle's hips as Danae used a scope to inspect its ears. So far, five hours of the work day were completed and no new threats appeared. Having to stand back and wait for instructions wasn't much different from what he'd done in the military. Sure, the team trained so their timing was right. But they'd also had long periods of waiting to gear up for a mission.

Last night, after he'd ended that kiss and endured her confused expression, Beck couldn't sleep. He figured he should have explained his reason, but he enjoyed getting to know her and didn't want her to look at him as anything but a whole man. He'd spent an hour studying the background file Hank supplied and verifying it with information he could find on the Internet. Hank's report was thorough. Beck figured she must have a clue about who was behind her current troubles.

While she slept, he'd snuck into her room to install a tracking device inside her cell phone. Hopefully, no situation would arise where it was needed, but he believed in being prepared for any possibility. On purpose, he'd avoided looking at the bed for fear he'd be tempted to crawl under the covers, next to her warm body.

"I got it." Danae straightened and held something on the end of a pair of thin forceps.

"Another foxtail?" The gray-haired man leaned forward in his chair.

"That's right, Mike." She scratched the brown and white dog under his chin. "Roger will be feeling better right away." She glanced at Beck and nodded.

Beck lifted the dog down to the floor.

The frisky dog ran to his owner.

"You rascal." Mike clipped a leash onto Roger's collar then stood. "I can't keep him out of the field behind our place."

"Understandable. Dogs are meant to roam. I'm glad the solution was an easy one." Danae escorted the man and dog to the reception area before returning to the counter and set the used instruments she'd used on a tray for delivery to the back room.

Her action was Beck's clue to grab the supplies and clean the table. He'd hoped to use these small breaks to ask her questions. Unfortunately, she was always focused on a task related to the previous client or the next. No denying her dedication was admirable, but not being proactive about gathering intel didn't sit well. He itched for something substantive that earned him a permanent spot on Hank's team.

The walkie-talkie on her hip squawked. "Doc, please pick up line two."

Danae moved into the procedure room and lifted the receiver from the wall phone. "Doctor Orestes speaking."

Beck followed and put his good ear near her head. From what he could understand, a dog struggled to birth a litter, her first one. Standing so close and smelling her citrusy scent was a distracting. He eased away and clasped his hands behind him. He'd heard enough to know the caller was known to the lady vet and not a threat.

She hung up. "We have to go to a ranch about ten miles away."

"Field trip." Grinning, he set the instrument tray near the autoclave, figuring Annie or Eric would find it."

Tapping a pen on the counter, she stared at the floor. "I've got an emergency kit in the vehicle. Let me check the schedule and give Eric whatever instructions are needed."

Beck pointed. "Do not leave the office. I'm going upstairs to change clothes and collect King."

Her brows scrunched. "Bringing him might not be the best choice. A strange dog near a birthing situation is not a good mix."

"Leaving him here is not an option. Let me worry about controlling my dog."

Fifteen minutes later, Beck steered the SUV off the highway north of Eagle Rock and onto a dirt and gravel road. Being out of those damned scrubs and doing something he was good at boosted his attitude. He'd insisted on driving, leaving her free to mentally prepare for the upcoming case.

A tan Jeep with out-of-state plates followed them for several blocks through town. It always stayed at least two car lengths back.

Beck's senses went on alert, and he tracked the vehicle's progress on the mirrors every few seconds but couldn't catch details about the out-of-state license.

Luckily, it turned off at the road leading to the freeway. "Where should I park?"

Danae's head popped up from focusing on her phone. "Shirley said Maisie's in a stall in the barn so there." She pointed past the red-painted ranch house.

"Will do." He eased the vehicle into the shade and cut the engine.

In the backseat, King stood and looked around.

Beck reached between the seats, unclipped the carabiner attached to the seat belt from the dog's harness, and rested a hand on King's shoulders. "*Stanna*, King. *Vakta*." While they were inside the barn, Beck intended King would guard the SUV and alert him to anyone's approach. He wasn't taking any chances on someone following them here and inflicting additional vandalism on her ride.

A brunette woman dressed in jeans and a plaid shirt rushed through the open barn door and gave an overhead wave. "Thank God, you're here. Hurry."

"Go to your patient, Danae." He squeezed her shoulder. "I'll grab your bag from the back." Moments later, he found the group by the sound of the woman's nervous chatter and set the bag where she could see it.

Danae knelt in the straw next to a mottled reddish-brown cattle dog. One hand rested on the dog's abdomen while she crooned nonsense words.

The dog kept jerking and bringing up her head to stare at her rear.

"Now, Shirley, I don't know if you want to stay here

for my exam." Danae opened her bag and quickly pulled on gloves then she unfolded a pad with plastic backing and set out instruments. "The first pup could be breech or transverse, so I'll have to reach in and turn it."

Beck's gut clenched. He didn't know if *he* wanted to be here.

"Can you get this muzzle on Maisie?" She thrust a dark object toward him.

"Uh, me?" A similar device was SOP when he and King rappelled down cliff faces or were lowered out of helicopters. He'd secured one on his own dog lots of times, but never on a strange dog.

"Please, Beck." Her lips pressed tight.

Pitching his voice low, he squatted by the dog's head and held out his left hand to let her sniff. "Good girl, Maisie."

The dog looked up with her dark eyes, pointed ears flicking forward then back, and gave a whimper.

He eased the muzzle over her nose and pinched the straps together behind her ears. Then he scratched under her chin before glancing back to see what came next.

Danae sat hunched over and peering with a flashlight through a device that stuck—

Ah, damn that was nasty. Beck looked away, not needing to be so involved with this process. The owner watched, but her face was pinched like she regretted choosing to stay.

Tires crunched on the dirt outside.

Beck stood and stepped back across the middle of the barn until he could see through the doorway, spotting a brown truck.

"Shirley, you inside?" A dark-haired man in slacks and sports coat rushed into the barn.

"We're here, Bob. Our poor Maisie is having a time of birthing."

Beck nodded as the man hurried by with a quirked eyebrow. Should have asked the lady if anyone else was expecting anyone. He waited for the other pet owner to enter the stall before he returned.

Danae removed the device and set it aside then she looked up until their gazes connected. "Beck, can I get your help?"

He heard the tension in her voice, but he doubted the owners noticed. Stepping close, he went down on one knee. "What's up?"

"The pup is breech, and I have to help it through the birth canal. Once it's born, it might need attention to get it breathing. I just need you ready to take on that task, if I have to focus on the next ones coming out."

The words came at him too fast. He'd been a volunteer intern for all of six and a half hours. What did he know about puppies? But her big brown eyes pleaded, and he just nodded, confident she'd explain in her thorough manner.

Then she turned to the owners. "Shirley, Bob, I know you want to be present. And I honor that wish.

But Maisie needs to be surrounded by calm energy right now. Can you manage that behavior, or would you like to wait just outside the barn?" As she talked, she stroked Maisie's side.

All he could do was marvel at her gentle nature with the dog and its owners. He pulled his phone from his hip pocket and searched on assisting puppy births.

Maisie tensed and whimpered, curling her head toward her rear.

Shirley gasped and touched the dog on her shoulder then her hip.

Bob stood and helped up Shirley. "We'll step outside, Danae, like you suggested."

Beck moved aside so they could pass. He watched a couple of videos with the sound off before returning his phone to his pocket.

With hands braced on her thighs, Danae took a deep breath and let it out slowly. Then she located a small syringe, squeezed in lubricating jelly, and inserted it inside the birth canal, depressing the plunger as she circled her hand.

Beck winced, his stomach jumping, but he couldn't look away.

"Come on, Maisie. You push, and I'll pull." She inserted two fingers. With her other hand, she stroked along the dog's ribs.

Years ago, he'd watched his father deliver calves and foals with the occasional stillbirth. 'What are the pup's chances?"

"Hard to say. Shirley wasn't sure how long Maisie had been laboring before she found her and called." Her eyes widened then she glanced toward the dog. "That's it, Maisie, don't fight the contraction."

Beck kept silent and just watched as Danae shifted and twisted her body so she pressed and gripped on the presenting legs. His admiration grew.

Finally, she sprawled on her belly. "Squeeze some jelly on this hand."

After stretching to reach the tube, Beck complied, noting he could see more of the pup.

"Get a towel ready. He's almost out."

Positioning his hands where he thought they were needed, he waited. She probably wasn't even aware she hummed a rhythmic chant under her breath as she tended the animal.

Maisie panted and moved her paws, rustling the straw.

Danae let out a whoop and set a limp blob into his hands. She scrambled to reach for a set of scissors to cut the sac and the umbilical cord.

Beck didn't feel any activity or see the pup's tiny chest moving. "He's not breathing."

"No, sometimes they revive." She pressed her pointer onto its chest with tiny jabs. "Rub the blanket against its body."

Side by side, they hovered over the pup that couldn't be more than five inches long. The air hung heavy around them, the August heat suddenly sweltering.

"Shouldn't you be breathing into its mouth, too?"

"Movies get it all wrong. I'd breathe mostly carbon dioxide into his tiny lungs."

Maisie whimpered, and Danae moved to the dog.

Beck rubbed, but he didn't hold out hope. The poor thing probably suffocated stuck inside.

"Move to where Maisie can lick him. But watch her." She held a towel at Maisie's rear.

He walked on his knees then laid the bundle in front of her. "Muzzle off?"

"Yes, and here's another."

Stretching to accept the second one, he rubbed it while giving an occasional glance at Maisie, who gave the damp lump a tentative lick. His attention centered on Danae's frantic movements as she caught two more puppies in less than five minutes. When he glanced back at Maisie, the pup was squirming under constant licking. Relief shot through him. "Hey, the first one's okay."

"Good. Put him on a nipple."

An instruction he'd never thought he'd hear. He did and then accepted the ones she passed over until four pups snuggled next to Maisie. Finally, the mother quit thrashing.

Moments later, he walked outside to tell the owners they could go be with Maisie. He stepped toward the SUV to check on King and spotted him curled up in the passenger seat. The sun must have just set, painting the underside of thin clouds above the Crazy Mountain a rosy pink.

His chest burned with the emotion of what he'd just experienced. That woman was amazing, so calm and assured under pressure, and he felt honored to have done what he could to assist.

Now, he had to earn his place within the ex-military men and women who made up the Brotherhood Protectors team. He had to put his own skills to work and figure out who threatened her.

CHAPTER 7

ON THE DRIVE BACK, Danae sat with her eyes closed, replaying Maisie's birth over and over in her head. What had she overlooked? Should she have done another X-ray on the sixtieth day of gestation to compare to the one done on the fifty-fifth? Would the breech have been spotted, or did the pup just flip with the onset of contractions?

A warm hand squeezed her forearm. She jumped and looked to the left. "What?"

"Don't beat yourself up."

She studied his profile, noting his balanced features that had become special in so short a time. "How did you know?'

"Because you're a professional, and you're looking for what you could have done better." He glanced to the side and winked. "I've been there and done that. Go back to the office, write up the incident, and then put it behind you. With the next whelping, you'll learn something different to store in your bag of tricks."

That comment produced a grin. "I have a bag of tricks?"

"Or whatever you call knowledge gained by experience."

His attitude was so good for her self-confidence. True she'd been practicing for less than a year and would face difficulties with any type of procedure. She would really hate finding out a technique existed that she didn't know about.

Beck punched on the radio then tapped a hand on the steering wheel in time with the beat.

"I'm hungry." She sat straighter. "What time is it?"

"Almost seven. Want to stop in town to eat?"

"Not at Al's again." She did a quick inventory of her refrigerator and cupboards. "I have ingredients for pasta primavera."

"That's vegetable pasta, right?" He turned right at the next intersection. "We're swinging by Tag's, so I can grab meat out of the freezer." He pulled into the driveway of a ranch-style house with muted light shining at the edges of the front window. The house sat at the end of a cul-de-sac with rail fencing that angled into the darkness on both sides. Beck unhooked King's harness then opened the door and stepped out. "You coming?"

"Beck, I've just come from a whelping." She waved a

hand at her front. "I'm sure I have birthing goo on my scrubs that would disgust your friend."

"Friends. I see Malin's car, too." He jerked a thumb over his shoulder. "Tag and I have worked with dogs for years. We know about *goo*. Come on."

Hearing her friend was inside, she shoved open the door.

Beck waited at the front of the SUV and reached out for her hand before heading up the walkway.

King scrambled out of the back seat and trotted toward the door.

Her skin warmed from where her hand disappeared into his larger one. The gesture lightened her heart, how he made the connection and kept her close. Once they got inside and she saw the couple on the couch together, she realized she had met Tag on one occasion in her office.

"Which one is this?" Danae perched on the edge of a sofa and scratched under the chin of a sweet tri-color Beagle in Malin's lap.

King and the Beagle touched noses then the Shepherd wandered away.

"Pixie's my therapy dog. Taffy has moved on to her permanent owner."

Danae studied her friend who appeared a lot more relaxed than the last time she saw her. Knowing better than to mention what Malin went through during the bank robbery, Danae looked for another topic. "Wow, your hair's grown a lot since you cut it."

Malin reached up a hand to her honey-blonde hair. "Yeah, and I'm loving every stage. I don't know if I'll ever grow it almost to my waist again." Then she turned and gave a narrowed-eyed glare. "Tag told me you're being stalked."

Her stomach crimped. *That word again.* "I wouldn't call what's happened stalking." She shrugged. "A crank call and slashed tires."

Shaking her head, Malin tsked. "At first, I denied the situation, too." She stroked a hand over Pixie's head. "Don't. Listen to what Beck tells you to do. And know I'm here to talk to, if you need it."

Her friend's words brought a lump to Danae's throat. *I must be more tired than I thought.* She could only nod.

"Got what I needed." Beck strode into the room holding a six-pack of beer and a foil-wrapped lump, with King on his heels. "Let's go cook some dinner."

Suddenly overcome with weariness, Danae pushed up then took a quick step to get her balance.

"Hey, you all right?" Frowning, Beck grabbed her elbow.

She forced a smile. "Just tired and hungry."

Ten minutes later, she unlocked the front door to the office, glancing around the space before she stepped inside. Everything looked all right. Out of habit, she went straight to the desk, searching for any notes left by employees.

As scheduled, the three pets—two being boarded

and one post-neuter—had been picked up. "Great, the kennel is empty tonight." She dragged her feet to the supply closet and grabbed a gallon of hydrogen peroxide and a bucket for soaking her scrubs. "I'm going upstairs and taking a shower."

Beck sat at the computer. "I'll be up to start dinner as soon as I review the security footage."

She opened her mouth to argue then snapped it shut. Why would she stop him? "Fine by me." She stepped under the stream of hot water tired and wanting to crawl into bed and emerged revitalized. As the jets of her massage showerhead worked out the kinks of her knotted muscles, she reviewed the accomplishment of handling her first difficult whelping. Sure, she'd read about the process but reading and doing were so very different.

Not wanting to take the time to dry her hair, she gathered it into a bun on the top of her head. Wearing yoga pants and a baggy long-sleeved shirt from college, she opened her door to the smell of frying onions and garlic—the beginning of so many wonderful dishes. She entered the kitchen under King's watchful eye, but the dog remained on the rag rug in front of the sink. "Smells great. What should I do?"

Beck glanced over his shoulder. "You'll probably want a salad."

"You don't?"

"I'll eat some if it's made, but I usually don't put one together myself."

"Huh, interesting." She peeked at her stove that had pots and pans on each burner. Beck managed them all. Her meals were usually simpler involving two burners at most.

The result was spectacular. The pasta retained the right amount of chewiness, and the sauce contained enough zing from the spices to make her lips tingle. Although, the whole time they ate and talked, she'd wished for a different reason to be aware of her lips. The moment he stood, she jumped up. "You cooked so I'll do the dishes."

"You sure?" He picked up the beer bottle.

"Absolutely." She rested a hand on his forearm and took the plate from his hand with the other. "The pasta was exactly what I needed. Thanks."

"Without the meat?" His eyebrow arched.

"I added hemp hearts for my protein." She turned to collect the other dishes and, in a minute, heard cheers from a sports event on the television. Although she hadn't named her disquieted feelings in recent months, she now recognized how the evenings were lonely before Beck's arrival.

At first, she had so much to do to get the business up and running. Now, she was glad for someone to talk to. As she set the clean dishes in the drying rack, she wondered how to bring up the topic of his hearing aid. Or did she even need to?

In the sitting room, she grabbed a professional journal from the stack under the end table and curled into a corner of the couch. Between paragraphs, she sneaked looks over the pages at Beck, who lounged with his legs extended. Her initial questions about his hearing kept bugging her.

"Do I pass inspection?"

She jerked. "What?"

"You're watching me."

"I was being stealthy."

"Danae, I was stationed in both Iraq and Afghanistan and have developed a sense when I'm being watched. Had to, in order to stay alive." He muted the TV and rolled his head on the sofa cushion to look her way. "What's up?"

"Today, when you were at the computer, I spotted your hearing device and am curious."

He lifted a hand and tugged his hair over his left ear. "What do you want to ask? If I'm adequate for the job of guarding you?" Scowling, he sat upright.

Ouch. His tone sure prickled. "I wondered if the injury happened at the same time as King's." She stretched to place a hand on his shoulder. "I don't doubt your ability, Beck."

"Thought I was better at hiding it." He stared straight ahead.

"All I noticed before this morning was a slight angled position in how you sat during conversations. A position which could have been caused by so many other physical issues."

He huffed out a breath and leaned forward, his

elbows planted on his thighs. "That damn mortar ended both King's and my military careers. I'll never be back at one hundred percent and have to salvage what I can to develop another career."

His expression looked carved from stone, and her heart ached. Not being a Ranger obviously weighed on him. But surely, he couldn't have served as one forever. What could she say? "In cases where one of the senses is hindered, the others get stronger. People who go blind develop more acute hearing and a finer sense of touch."

"Huh." He stared at the flashing images on the TV screen.

"I'll bet you've unconsciously learned to read lips."

"I doubt that. Won't help get me back in the field."

His retort felt like a slap, but she refused to let it deter her. "Let's test my theory. Watch my mouth and tell me what I said." With precise movements, she mouthed, King is a great dog.

"Do it again." He braced a hand in the middle sofa cushion and leaned close.

A bit unnerved by the directness of his stare on her mouth, she repeated her statement.

"Shit, that movement looks sexy as hell." In a quick action, he crawled close and pinned her to the corner of the sofa with his chest. His intense gaze focused on her mouth. "Those moves are such a tease."

Her pulse raced. Every bit of her femaleness wanted to respond to the intimate pose and the primal look in his half-closed eyes. But, she needed to know what she'd started out to learn and held him inches away with a stiffened forearm across his chest. "But did you understand?"

"You said, King is a great dog." A grin flashed then he lowered his head.

She melted under the hard, possessive kiss, cupping her hands on his strong jaw. Not wanting him to end this sensual delight, she vowing not to lift them higher.

He sucked her lower lip into his mouth and pressed a hand on her hip.

His mouth tasted of spicy sauce and tangy beer, and she swept her tongue inside for more. More heat. More tension. More of Beck. Their questing tongues speared then soothed, lapped then lunged.

He eased kisses over her jaw and onto her neck.

Goose bumps rose on her skin, and she linked her hands behind his neck. "Hmm."

Tightening the embrace, he scooted them level on the cushions with him lying on his left side. His hand stroked her shoulder, her ribs, and her hips in rapid succession.

Danae tasted the underside of his jaw and the strong column along the side of his neck. Every place she touched was taut skin over solid muscle.

Beck teased his fingers under the hem of her sweatshirt and grazed the tips over her belly. "I've got to touch you."

For a fleeting second, she wondered how wise

taking the next step was. Then she was lost to the sensation of him plucking her nipple until it puckered and tingled. She wiggled and slid a thigh between his knees. But the position of them squished together on the sofa was too confining. "My bedroom is only a few feet away."

"Wasn't entering without an invitation."

She rolled away, braced a hand on the floor, and stood. "Consider yourself invited." As she walked down the hall, she thought of what she had to move to make things tidy. A strong arm wrapped around her middle from behind, and that worry flew out of her head as his heat invaded her body.

Beck aligned their legs and mirrored the last few steps into the bedroom. He moved a leg and closed the door behind them.

A faint click of dog toenails drew closer, followed by the clunk of a big dog lying on a wooden floor.

"Get naked." Beck yanked his T-shirt over his head and tossed it aside then unbuttoning the waistband of his jeans.

The waxing moon allowed enough light for her to enjoy another look at his sculpted body. She shimmied out of her yoga pants, sliding off her panties in the same motion. Self-conscious about her too-small breasts, she pulled the shirt over her head and hurried under the covers.

Beck sat on the edge of the mattress, muscles bunching and releasing as he untied his boots. He paused and glanced over his shoulder. "Need you to know I tested clean on my discharge physical."

The conversation was one she hadn't needed to have in over five years. Heat inflamed her cheeks, and she hoped he wouldn't notice. She gripped the sheet tighter under her chin. "I haven't been with anyone since my divorce, and my IUD is still in place."

After moving a hand to his ear then to the night-stand, he stood and shucked his jeans before tossing back the quilt. "Won't need anything to get tangled in."

Then she was delightfully accosted by a warm body and caressing touches. He skimmed his hands over her skin like a sculptor—kneading, molding, smoothing. Every nerve ending came alive, and arousal zinged in a path following his strokes. She rubbed her fingers over the ridges of his shoulders and the hard planes of his chest, enjoying the light abrasion of wiry hairs. She sucked in a deep breath and wiggled her nipples across his pecs.

"Again." He nuzzled behind her ear and reached up a hand to pull out the scrunchie.

She complied and was rewarded with a low groan and the press of his hard shaft against her hip. Exploring his abdominals produced raspy breathing from them both.

Beck levered up to balance on an elbow and ran his fingers through her hair, spreading it across the pillow. "I've thought about your hair."

"You have?"

"I want you to swing the ends of it over my belly. But right now, I need to be inside you." His knee pressed against her thighs.

Hitching her breath, she let him work her legs apart, expecting him to move between them. Instead, he explored the sensitive skin of her inner thighs, just grazing fingertips in lazy circles before they rose to play with her feminine curls.

He leaned down and took a nipple between his lips, rolling his tongue around the tip then sucking it against the roof of his mouth.

She arched off the mattress, wanting more, then stayed bowed as his fingers slid between her folds. When a single, broad finger entered her, she squealed. The pleasure was already building fast.

"I want to make the climb together." He withdrew and tickled her engorged nub, nibbling kisses along her neck.

Need pulled at her belly, and her skin felt alive. "What if I want you hard and fast?"

He lifted his head and gave a lop-sided grin. "At your command."

The statement seemed a bit much. She'd never ordered anyone in her life. But then she got a look at him...all of him. The sight was amazing. A fit male with not an inch of visible body fat and an impressive erection held himself over her body. At the moment he pressed the tip of his shaft against her sex, she did feel a little in command. That feeling lasted only until he pressed inside in a slow glide, and her body's instincts took over.

She ran her hands over his chest and belly, rubbing her fingertips across the ends of his taut nipples. His hard, solid body made her feel secure. Would saying so scare him away?

"So tight." Beck stroked and retreated, using bold caresses to mold and squeeze her breast.

She wanted to enjoy a slow-burn arousal, but she also needed to be filled to the limit to know she was not alone. At that last thought, her eyes flipped wide. Was she using him for the wrong reason?

Then he increased the rhythm of his strokes, filling her followed by grinding in a circle before he retreated.

Clamping her hands on his shoulders, she strained to meet each thrust, shivers of arousal running along her skin. Her blood sang in her veins. If she timed her move right, she could lick a nipple or his sternum when he thrusted upward. The first wave of her orgasm hit and all she could do was wrap her legs around his hips and hold on for the ride. "All the way inside. Fill me."

Beck plunged inside over and over, his breath harsh in his throat. "No argument here."

The iron bed frame bumped against the wall with steady beats.

Hot breaths wafted over her face. Tingles made her nether lips contract and she bit her lower lip, anticipating a blissful release.

Then he stopped and rested his forehead on her shoulder. "I'm not feeling you enough."

Her mouth was too dry to form a complete sentence. "Huh?"

"Hold tight." He levered upward to a kneeling position with her still wrapped around his shoulders and hips. Then he eased down until he balanced his butt on his heels with her in his lap, bracing his hands on her hips.

With his penis so deep, she was stretched until her channel tingled with a delicious burn. Digging her toes into the mattress and flexing her thighs boosted the pressure.

Beck moved her in languid glides along his length, his intense gaze focused as he increased the pace.

Lost in the clear depths of his blue eyes, she rode him in a rhythm that settled over their bodies until they breathed the same heated air and smelled the same tangy scents of their combined arousal. The friction drove her wild, and she arched back to plant a hand on his knee to provide leverage to meet his thrusts. So close, she soared, her muscles taut and expectant. His breaths puffed against her breasts, pearling her nipples tighter.

Beck wrapped an arm around her back and the other one low on her hips, still guiding her movements.

The grinding of coarse hairs on her sensitized bud sent her over the edge, and she convulsed, rasping out her orgasm in panting sighs. Then her body just floated, hanging limp in his embrace. Nipping kisses trailed down her neck as he loosened his hold and eased her back.

Still seated deep inside, Beck curled his body to lave her breasts with strong licks and gently tease her nipples with the edge of his teeth.

The touches sparked her energy. She revived enough to cup a hand on his shoulder and dig in her fingers. How he kept them together she didn't know, but he stretched above her, and she had to grab an iron rail to anchor herself against his deep plunges. Air gusted from her parted lips. Blood pumped in her ears. She stared at the hardening planes of his face, catching the moment he teetered on the edge before he gave two more thrusts then went his body went rock hard. The only part that moved was his shaft as it pumped out his release.

Then his arms gave way and he relaxed on top of her.

Perspiration dampened tendrils to her cheeks. His weight crushed her, but the feeling of this brawny man between her and the rest of the world was comforting...for about ten seconds. Then she had to breathe and tapped him on the shoulder. "Off."

Groaning, he rolled to the side but kept an arm at her waist. "Give me a few minutes."

She stroked a finger over his eyebrows as he rested. "For what?"

"For a second go." His eyelids fluttered but didn't open.

Danae cuddled close, playing with the ends of his hair, content to listen to the beat of his heart and hear the steady in and out of his breath. For now, she'd cherish this closeness. Because when he held her like this within the circle of his strong arms, with her head pillowed on his rounded shoulder, she could almost forget the real reason he came into her life.

Almost.

CHAPTER 8

THE NEXT TWO days were routine enough that Beck grew bored. He stood off to the side of the exam table as Danae checked in the ears of a tiny fluffy dog. His help wasn't needed, and his thoughts drifted.

Nothing out of the ordinary showed up on the security camera footage besides the usual wildlife. The clients Danae saw were for routine vaccinations, check-ups, and minor procedures. He thought he'd done a good job of hiding his aversion to needles, but when they were alone, she teased him about the faces he made.

The major payoff of boring days was Danae having energy for after-work activities. One night, they went to the Blue Moose and danced for an hour then relaxed and listened to the band. He'd watched for the suspicious Jeep on the road and cruised the lot at the tavern looking for it before he parked his truck. But nothing.

Yesterday, they drove out to Larry's farm again to practice lure coursing. He jogged through a just-plowed field with King while Danae dribbled a god-awful-smelling concoction that a hunter client swore would put any scent dog onto a trail. The plan was for her to follow the wire for part of the track then veer off in an opposite direction.

They'd stood, hands gripped tight, watching King's progress.

"Another fifty feet or so." She bounced on the balls of her feet.

So much rode on King getting back his tracking ability. Beck held his breath as he watched his dog lope after the flapping bag then jerk up his head and veer off to the left. "Hot damn, he did it." He scooped up Danae and plastered kisses on her soft cheeks, nose, and forehead, saving the best spot for last.

The best thing that happened over the past two nights was the sex. Their connection was strong and fiery. She'd fulfilled his fantasy of swishing her long hair over not only his chest but just about every other inch of his body. Snapping his head toward the sound of his name, he straightened. "Sorry, what's that?"

"The cleaning." Danae waved a hand toward the empty table. "You had a telling grin. Like you remembered—"

"Don't ask." He kept the bulging front of his scrubs turned away as he retrieved the cleaning supplies and faced the table.

Tapping sounded on the door a moment before Annie stuck in her head. "Uh, Danae, a man just arrived and wants to see you."

"An emergency? For which pet?" She looked up from where she wrote in a folder.

"None." Biting her lip, she glanced at Beck then slipped inside and pressed the door closed. "Says he's your husband and demands your presence."

Suspicion over the timing of this man's appearance raised the hairs on Beck's neck. The word "demand" didn't sit well.

Danae stiffened. "Giles is here?"

Beck stopped scrubbing the towel over the metal and watched the emotions cross her face. After shock came fear that quickly morphed to irritation. He could understand shock and irritation, but why fear?

In his mind, he stepped closer, hoping she knew he was there to support her. In practice, he kept his distance so the dynamics of supervisor and intern were maintained.

"What's the next appointment?" Danae tapped the end of her pen against the counter.

"An exam for heartworm on Aggie, the McLaughlins' Basset."

She frowned, tapping the pen faster. "Where's Eric?"

Beck gave the table a final spray and dried the area, listening to the tense note in Danae's voice. She was really bugged by this man's presence. Maybe he better check out this guy for himself.

The blonde jerked her head toward the wall. "Deworming a litter of kittens in the other room."

Danae huffed out a breath. "Show my *ex-husband* to my office and tell him I'll be there in fifteen minutes."

Annie turned then paused. "You never said how handsome he is."

"Annie, just go."

When the door closed, Beck stepped close and set a hand on her rigid back. "You okay?"

"I just can't imagine why he traveled here. I haven't heard a word from him since the divorce, so why now?" She leaned a shoulder against his chest.

"Want me to go beat him up and send him packing?" Beck was only half kidding. The presence of a man who had been an important part of her life, knowing her intimately enough to have been married, brought out a burning jealousy that Beck never knew he possessed.

"Tempting." She glanced up and smiled. "But no. I will handle him."

Logical answer, but he didn't like it. "Know I'm here if you need backup."

"I do." Stretching up on tiptoes, she brushed a kiss on his lips.

Beck fought the urge to sweep her into an embrace and stretch her flat on the newly clean table.

She eased away and gathered the folder then stepped through the back door.

A glance around informed him the room was ready for the next appointment. He grabbed the sack with the wet rags from under the counter and walked into the reception area. Normally, the rags weren't delivered to the laundry room until the end of the day. But they provided a plausible reason to stroll past Danae's office.

He kept his gaze straight ahead as he walked down the hallway, only giving one sideways glance as he passed the doorway. The jerk had the balls to sit in her chair and rifle through her desk drawers. The bag rustled as his grip tightened.

After dropping the dirty towels on the washing machine, he turned and sauntered into her office. "Excuse me, sir."

The man with wavy dark hair and heavy beard stubble jerked around.

"Is the doctor aware you're snooping?" Through the lingering haze of spicy cologne, he walked to the bookshelf on the far wall and ran a finger along the spines before glancing over his shoulder.

"I don't snoop." He stood and adjusted the sleeves of his suit jacket. "I'm family and have a right to check on what's happening in Danae's life." The drawer shut with a slam.

The man's arrogant tone grated, but Beck refused to engage in a pissing match. Danae didn't need the aggravation. Instead, he pulled out the next volume he touched. "Interesting." He met the man's dark-eyed gaze, registering the tick of a muscle at the corner of his left eye. The guy, who might be an inch taller but weighed twenty to twenty-five pounds less, wore expensive slacks and a jacket, but the shirt was a silky, crew-necked tee. Around his neck hung a gold chain, the color matching a watch on his left wrist. "Most people who claim to be family don't look through another family member's drawers." He made a point of glancing at the desk before turning with a shrug.

He walked around to the procedure room then entered the dog exam room and set the book on the counter.

Danae glanced between him and the book with an eyebrow raised.

Knowing the explanation was too involved, he smiled at the pet owner then pretended interest in whatever Danae did with the big dog lying on the table. Looked too heavy for her to lift. He really should have been here when the dog was brought in.

The skin on the back of his neck itched. He couldn't reconcile the man in her office with someone Danae would be interested in. Why would a person Danae hadn't seen in at least six months show up with no notice and search her office? Presumably, when they divorced, they cut all ties—personally and financially.

The more he thought about the situation the angrier he got. What had she first seen in the guy? She didn't live an expensive lifestyle, but he'd bet that everything her ex owned carried a designer label. Hell, seeing what vehicle the out-of-towner rented would be the clincher.

"Beck, I need your help."

He jerked to attention and stepped around behind her until he stood on the opposite side of the table. "With what?"

"Please hold Aggie's collar and slip a hand under her chest to encourage her to stand." She adopted the described position then leaned over the dog's back. "Quit glaring. You're scaring the owner."

Unclenching his jaw, he watched for her short nod to assist the dog onto her feet. He stayed at the side of the table until the exam was over then he lifted the basset down to the floor. Debate rambled through his mind over sharing what he'd seen. He decided to keep quiet, because he didn't want the interloper to known Beck reported on the guy's activities.

But damn, he wished he'd brought a bugging device from Hank's to install in the office.

DANAE WASHED her hands again then leaned a hip on the counter as she dried them. Every pertinent detail related to the last patient's case had been dealt with. The afternoon's schedule had been forgotten with the new of Giles' arrival. *What is he doing here? How does he*

know where I live? She gave her reflection a glance in the bathroom mirror. A few tendrils hung loose from her ponytail, but she wasn't about to primp for her ex. Getting this conversation over with was the only way to get him out of her office and her life…again.

Walking down the hallway, Danae didn't glance at Annie. Let the woman drool over Giles Charonopoulos' handsome exterior. The man's interior was twisted and ugly. At the doorway, she stopped short, bristling at the sight of Giles leaning back with his Italian loafers resting on top of today's mail. *The gall.* "Get out of my chair."

"Finally. Do you know how long I've waited?" He dropped his feet then stood and ran both hands down the front of his trousers.

"A situation you should have expected when you dropped by unannounced."

"Χρόνια πολλά, Danae, darling!"

Many years--the ubiquitous Greek greeting meant for any and every occasion. She ignored his broad smile and leaned back to evade his outstretched arms, waiting until he exited her space. A glance at her desk's surface clued her that he'd moved just about every item.

"You refuse a familial greeting?" He shot her a sideways look from under his heavy brows.

"Since we're no longer related, I do." Had she really thought that look was charming when they first met? She plopped down into her chair and flexed her ankles.

"What do you want, Giles? I have more patients arriving this afternoon."

"I'd say you're looking well, but you're really not. That lab coat does nothing for your figure. And what adult woman wears her hair in such a style?" He waved a dismissive hand as he sat and crossed an ankle over the opposite knee.

Should she bother answering or just wait him out? But as always, his comments about her appearance hit hard. "My attire and hairstyle are functional for the duties I perform."

"Your family sends their greetings." He glanced around. "You'll give me a complete tour, of course. Your father especially asked me to determine if he needs to insist on you returning home."

Although the thought rankled, she really wasn't surprised. The men in her family had always acted like they knew what was best for everyone. She leaned back in her chair. With restraint, she kept from crossing her arms over her chest—but just barely.

From the corner of her eye, she spotted movement as King entered and sat three feet away from Giles. At the thought of Beck sending in reinforcements, she bit back a smile. Her heart warmed.

"You allow beast-like dogs to roam the premises?" Eyes wide, he grabbed the armrests and set both feet on the floor. "What is that animal doing in here?"

He'd had a bad experience with a dog as a child and would never let her have a pet during their marriage. A smile threatened to erupt. "Not usually, but King is a special case." She snapped her fingers. "King, *komma*."

King's head jerked around and he watched her for a second or two before he obeyed.

"This dog is ex-military and earned a commendation for his brave service abroad." She rubbed fingers the length of King's ears. Her statement might be stretching the truth. Why not set her ex's imagination going? "Again, Giles, I ask why are you here?"

"I have business in the area."

A muscle at the corner of his eye ticked. His tell, guaranteeing that what followed would all be lies. "Montana doesn't have any ports." One of the reasons why she picked this state.

"Well, I'm on my way to Seattle. But that's not the real reason." He scooted forward in the chair.

Booking a direct flight from Philadelphia to Seattle had to be easier than coming to Bozeman then renting a car. But she made sure not to let her expression display her skepticism. She pulled away her hand and leaned back in the chair.

King moved to the corner of the desk and stared.

"At a recent family wedding, I was cornered by Aunt Odessa."

She lifted her eyebrows for dramatic effect. "Oh, who got married?" How far would he carry this ruse?

He ran a hand through his hair, which left a black tuft curled over his forehead. "Uh, a cousin you never met. Aunt Odessa inquired about that amethyst necklace. You know, the one in the scrollwork setting." He cleared his throat and glanced at King. "She wanted to make sure the jewelry stayed in the family. An heirloom, you know."

His voice held the supercilious tone she'd heard so many times at business dinners, and her stomach knotted. "But you told me you bought the pendant during a business trip to Mykonos." Nothing of what he said added up. His loose grasp of the truth had caused lots of problems in their relationship. He contended the laissez-faire attitude was essential to negotiate complicated business contracts. She appreciated the fact she no longer had to worry about sifting through what he said to find the kernel of truth.

"Maybe I've mixed up the one she meant." He smiled, flashing his even white teeth. "Why don't we look through your jewelry case? I'll know the piece when I see it."

The idea of him upstairs in her personal space made her shudder. "Sorry, that's not happening. You didn't contest the division of property nine months ago, and the judge proclaimed the listing I presented as final."

"Now, now, Danae." He stood and leaned over the front of her desk, eyes narrowed. "What happened to that sweet, compliant girl I wooed?"

His gaze was hard as obsidian, but she didn't flinch. "Back to the subtle insults?"

"Insult, no." His gaze shifted to the side and back. Then he smiled wide enough to crinkle the skin at his eyes. "I came to tell you that I've missed you. The apartment is too quiet."

"Did Stavros and Nestor move out?"

"No." His eyes rounded. "I need my security detail. A man of my importance must take precautions."

Feeling the conversation was going nowhere, she pushed to her feet.

King circled from where he'd sat to settle at her side.

"Giles, I have patients to see, and I don't think we have anything else to say to each other."

"What if I told you I wanted you back?" He scrambled toward the side of the desk and extended a hand, palm up.

King snapped to his feet, ears pricked toward the stranger.

Unable to restrain herself, she scoffed. "You didn't act like you wanted me when we were married, so what's changed?" She shook her head. "Scratch that. What I should have said is, I have no need for you in my life. Tell Father my practice is growing, and I've made new friends here."

"How can you compare this…" He frowned and waved a hand over his head. "Rustic building in the middle of nowhere with what I provided for you back home?"

"Easy." The tension that had been building lessened. This conversation resolved any tiny inkling of doubt she'd ever entertained over her decision. "Here, I'm the one in control of my life, and now, I make my own decisions."

His dark brows crashed down. He glared then shook his head. "We'll see how long that lasts." Following another narrow-eyed stare, he stomped out of the room.

The tension returned and pounded in her temples. She slumped into her chair and stared at the empty doorway.

What did Giles mean?

CHAPTER 9

BECK DROVE BACK toward the vet's office, hoping he wouldn't get pulled over for speeding. As soon as Danae left to talk to her asshole of an ex, he'd collected King from the temporary crate they used during business hours and let him loose at the foot of the stairs. Then he'd memorized the license plate and rental agency from the burgundy late-model, full-size luxury car as he headed toward his truck.

Once the road turned into the foothills, he'd pushed his twelve-year old truck to its limits to reach White Oak Ranch and collected specialized electronics from Hank's inventory. Everything about the too-suave, too-assured businessman screamed trouble, and Beck wanted to have every possible precaution in place.

Only a mile or so from the vet's office, he spotted the same sedan heading toward town. The scowl on the jerk's face as he sped by told the whole story. He'd arrived looking for an admission or concession of some type but was leaving without getting what he wanted. *Way to go, Danae.* Beck pumped a congratulatory fist in the air. Hopefully, she'd want to share details when they had a moment to themselves.

Hours later, Beck shoved the dirty towels into the washing machine and started the cycle. He walked to Danae's office door and looked inside, spotting King circled up a couple feet inside the room.

The doc sat with her hands poised above the keyboard, but she stared into space.

He rapped his knuckles on the door frame.

Danae started then glanced his way.

"You about done here?" He disliked seeing the tired slump of her shoulders.

"I'm not getting anything accomplished so I might as well quit." She clicked a few keys then lowered the laptop lid. "Any chores remain?"

"Everything's set for the morning. As soon as we change clothes, I'll bring down our scrubs and toss them in the washer."

Nodding, she flashed a smile then trudged up the stairs.

Beck kept quiet, waiting for her to share what had her so distracted. Ten minutes later, he sprawled at one end of the couch with a half-finished beer balanced on the upholstered armrest. He flicked between a couple baseball games to see which one sparked his interest. Standing around and doing nothing for the bulk of the day took more energy than he would have imagined.

Danae walked into the room, dropped onto the sofa sideways, and pulled up her legs. "I can't figure out this situation."

He muted the volume. "What situation?" *As if I don't know.*

"The reason Giles showed up today." She pulled up a heel to rest on the top of her opposite knee.

Position looks painful. Beck turned a bland expression her way, hoping she'd continue.

"He said he was here at my father's behest, but the specific item he asked about dealt with his family." She lifted her linked hands over her head and stretched to the side. "I looked in my bedroom and didn't find what he was asking about. Probably inside a box in the shed."

"Mind telling me what he said?"

"He asked about a necklace he gave me. Now he says it's a family heirloom, but when he gave it to me, he said he picked it up on a business trip."

"So he mixed up two pieces of jewelry. Doesn't sound like a big deal." The man might have been too smooth for Beck's tastes, but the issue sounded like standard post-divorce haggling. He glanced at the TV, but a commercial was on.

"Except twice, he asked to see the upstairs. And he mentioned my jewelry case. That's odd because I think most people call it a jewelry box."

He shrugged. *What is she getting at?*

"Not asking particulars here, but think about your last serious relationship. Did you know where your last lady friend stored her earrings and necklaces?"

"Why would I care about that detail?"

"Exactly." She grinned. "Why would Giles want to see my jewelry case?"

Beck stilled then turned to face her. "Because he put something inside that you now have."

Her gut clenched. Could that be true? "I need to search for that case in the shed."

He stood, extended a hand, and pulled her to her feet. They tromped down the stairs and into the backyard in a flash.

Danae worked the combination lock, and then reached inside to pull the chain on the overhead battery light. "In this notebook is a listing of what's inside each box. We're looking for boxes marked 'B' for bedroom." She held the open book toward the light and ran a finger down the neat printing.

Beck shoved a hand through his hair. He'd never seen such organization. Whenever he moved, he wrapped his clothes in a couple of sheets and jammed the rest of his belongings in duffles.

"Look for B-five. A small box, so probably it's on an upper shelf."

He stepped past her and reached down the marked box. "Here, or in the house?"

"Might as well take it inside. Time for me to put more stuff away."

At the receptionist desk, she stripped off the tape and dug in. Mementos and a photo cube went to one side before she lifted out the leather case, working the zipper around the circumference. "Here's the piece Giles asked about."

Beck held out his hand to receive the purple pendant then held it up toward the light. Nothing unusual about the stone.

Danae dumped out bracelets and rings, giving them only a cursory look. "I recognize everything here. Maybe he was just playing one of his mental games."

"Look deeper." Beck hated that she had someone in her life who messed with her confidence like this guy had. "Does the case have a second layer? I remember my mom's had a tray that lifted out."

She stepped back. "I don't see it, but maybe you will."

The permission he'd been waiting for. He lifted the container to the counter and turned it so he could view it from all angles. One of the upper corners appeared looser than the others. He pressed along the edge and worked out a small flash drive.

Her eyes rounded. "That's not mine."

"Exactly." He extended it. "Let's see what he was trying to recover."

"Now the phone call makes sense." Danae sat at the computer and typed.

"You never said, so I assume the caller mentioned giving up an item." Beck caught her nod then moved behind her and leaned a hand on the back of the chair. The list of files appeared as a bunch of spreadsheets."Do you know what you're looking at?"

"No. I just recognize names he mentioned or people I met at business dinners." She leaned close, manipulating the mouse, and the images on the screen flicked between two files. "This file relates to my father's business but is almost the same as this one." The image changed.

"An individual file per client." Beck pointed. "Look at the totals at the bottom. Different by a hundred thousand in this one and three hundred thousand in another."

"Multiple accounts. He's stealing from my father's company, I can't believe it, after all Father did for his career by bringing him into the business." She jumped to her feet. "I don't want this nasty thing in my house."

"See this notation." He slid into the vacated chair. "That's a classification for a military weapon that several Ranger teams field-tested while I was in Afghanistan. We all rejected the unit as unreliable and unsafe. These accountings with differing amounts point toward money laundering." Beck rubbed a hand over his jaw. "If he's being investigated, these spreadsheets are evidence."

She paced. "My older brother, Dion, would know, but we haven't spoken since I left Pennsylvania. He's very traditional and opposed my divorce."

Beck pulled out his phone and snapped pictures of

the case. "Hank will know where to send it. Write a statement with a timeline of all the details about when you packed up this case, when your ex last had access, and when you left home. Then explain why both of our fingerprints are on the device."

Two hours later, they climbed the flight of stairs after returning from an FBI field office in Bozeman. There, they handed over their signed statements and the flash drive to an agent who Beck swore had just graduated college.

On the drive back, he'd introduced other topics, but she didn't respond. He watched Danae withdraw into herself and wished he knew how to reach her. What he wanted was to bury himself deep into her warmth so she'd forget this mess and feel alive and connected.

Or maybe that's what he needed.

He suspected she'd want to be alone tonight, but he hated the idea she'd walk into her bedroom and close the door, locking him out. "Are you gonna say anything, Danae? The guy is scum, and you need to forget about him."

"I know." She stepped close and rested a hand on his chest. "I'm just sad."

His chest pinched, because he'd never seen her so... resigned. He covered her hand with his and pressed them against his chest. "Let me hold you. No sex."

~

"WRONG." Danae looked into Beck's too-serious expression and saw his worry and caring. She twisted her fingers to grasp his hand and tugged him toward her bedroom. "I want you. I want the night to end with different memories." Inside the room, she shed clothes as she walked to the bed.

Turning over the flash drive could bring troubles for her father's business, but she saw it as a way to distance themselves from Giles' mess. Her action was an attempt to fix the breach with the family. The evidence backed up what she'd told them about her suspicions that Giles dealt with unsavory people. Her father and brothers always hushed her, insisting they were in charge and would handle the details.

When her body hit the cool sheets, she pushed away all negative thoughts. On her side, she reached for Beck's strength as he slid beside her. In an instant, she grabbed his face and showered him with kisses. An urgency she didn't really understand drove her. Her skin tingled with growing arousal. She reached down to test his readiness, stroking his erection until it pulsed in her hand.

"Slow down, Danae." Beck nuzzled along her jaw.

"I want you."

"Same here, but not in the next nanosecond." His hand brushed across her breast, fingers drawing a circle on her flesh.

She arched forward, hoping to send the message for him to grab her. Frustration welled. She needed him to take control and make her forget. "Harder." Her hands moved everywhere—neck, shoulders, chest, abdomen —firing her own excitement by touching his straining body and feeling his reaction.

With a moan, she shoved him to his back and climbed astride, centering her sex over the tip of his shaft. Then, with her hands braced near his shoulders, she lowered herself and let out a long breath.

Safe.

Rocking forward and back, she drew his length deep into her channel. With a flexing of her hips, she started a rhythm aided by Beck's hands on her hips.

Security.

Their movements weren't elegant, but instinct ruled their bodies as they pushed, pulled, groped, caressed, kissed, and nibbled to express their feelings and entice the other toward climax.

Danae knew she tried too hard. After the first rush, she couldn't heighten the arousal past a low boil. Doubt about what she'd done hit. Her body made the right moves, but her focus wasn't on the giving man who'd supported her. A warm palm cupped her cheek.

"Hey, where are you?"

She flopped onto his damp chest, chagrined that she'd started something she couldn't finish. "Sorry. I'm more upset than I thought."

Beck drew circles on her back. "Ready to try something else?" He kissed the top of her head.

She thought of feeling his mouth on her sex, of how

good he could make her feel, and pressed her thighs tight. "I wanted us connected."

"We will be." He sat up and eased her off his erection. "Get on your hands and knees."

Not exactly what she had in mind. But, from the moment he slid inside, her body responded. Her nipples peaked. She dug in her fingers and locked her elbows to keep resistance against each of his strokes.

He clamped a hand on her right hip.

Beck was so deep inside she could only think of the sensations of plunging friction and being filled with heat. Goose bumps rising on her skin signaled she was close, but for this position, she couldn't gauge his arousal.

Leaning on one hand, she clasped the freed one on his flexing hip to connect. Blood roared in her ears as her orgasm hit with a blast, quivering from her core to her fingertips. She dropped to her elbows to push back against his pounding strokes. Air whooshed from her parted lips.

Beck stilled. He groaned low in his throat, and a moment later, he rubbed a circle on her hip. "You okay?" His weight landed hard on the mattress.

Bouncing, she landed next to him and smiled at being enveloped in his embrace. "I'm fine." He'd claimed her usual side of the bed, but she didn't complain. Her muscles felt like warm jelly and all she wanted was to prolong the floaty, sated feeling.

Home.

From a sex-drugged sleep, Danae started at the first sharp bark. She rubbed a hand over her face and blinked in the dim room, with no idea of the time.

The barking came again, this time closer.

Strange. King didn't often bark. Beck said he was trained to keep quiet. Wrapped in his arms, she could barely move. *Why am I awake, but* his *dog is the one making noise?* Then she realized Beck had turned them in their sleep and his good ear was buried. She wiggled her shoulders.

He mumbled and tightened his hold, burying his nose at the back of her neck.

King scratched under the bedroom door. His bark now high-pitched.

A warning. Her pulse quickened. Danae tapped her foot against his shin and moved her head. Jeez, he was strong. "Beck." She pried at his hands to ease them open. "Beck!"

He sat upright, his body tensed. "What?"

King kept barking.

Beck jumped from bed and pulled on his clothes. "Stay here. I'll see what's going on."

He dashed from the room before she could say a word. The sound of running paws and footsteps compelled her to jump out of bed and drag on a set of sweats. She grabbed her phone from the charger, although she had no idea where Beck's was. At least clothed, she felt less vulnerable as she moved to the back window. What could have caused this mess?

CHAPTER 10

"*God hund*, King." Beck spotted the glow and flicker of flames before he even reached the staircase. He ran to the reception area and grabbed the fire extinguisher before bursting out the back door at a run. The roof of the shed was engulfed. From below, he extended his arms and sprayed foam on the edges to keep the fire from spreading down the walls. Then he grabbed a garden hose and smoldered the rest.

Nose to the ground, King circled the building before veering toward the base of a sprawling tree.

Vaguely, Beck registered King in tracking mode. But he pondered over the unlikely coincidence of their search in the shed earlier and a fire targeting that same spot.

Had someone watched them? Was her ex-husband's visit just to provoke her to set a trail toward what he wanted to retrieve? Wispy smoke rose from the roof, signaling the flames were gone.

If someone wanted to destroy the shed, wouldn't they start the fire at the bottom of the structure? His blood chilled.

Danae.

How could he have been so stupid? He dropped the hose and sprinted toward the house, stopping with a hand on the newel post. Damn, why hadn't he grabbed the hearing aid? "Danae!" He waited two seconds, turning his head to listen for any sound from upstairs. "Danae, answer me."

A scuffle sounded on this floor. With his back to the wall, he crept down the hallway. Shit, he felt naked without a weapon. Nobody in her office, and reception was empty. He didn't waste time looking in the exam rooms. At the bathroom, he ducked his head around the corner and spotted her.

Wide-eyed and gagged, she was being pulled halfway out the side door.

A masked person gripped her waist with an arm and pressed a gun to her temple. "Don't be a hero, soldier boy."

The voice was unidentifiable. His instinct told him to rush the guy, but the distance was too far to ensure her safety. Clenching both hands, he could do nothing but stare into her frightened eyes. He held her gaze, not daring to blink. Even a hallway away, her fear churned his gut. "I'll find you. Stay strong."

Then she was gone, and by the time he reached the door, all he saw were red tail lights disappearing down the road. Two people must have been involved.

Frustration threatened to sweep away rationality. Head bent and with hands on hips, he hauled in a deep breath. His brain went into Ranger mode, mentally clicking through the development of a plan. Goal one: recover Danae. Goals two: capture the bogies. Assets: KA-BAR knife, shotgun. Allies: King, Tag, Hank.

Within ten minutes, he'd rousted Tag, who readied the gear at his place, and contacted Hank, who sprang into action to loop in the sheriff and put his helicopter pilot on standby. Based on the still-moving signal from her phone, Beck guessed she was being taken into the mountains to a hunting cabin.

Arriving at the house, he found Tag in the garage with both of their Ranger duffle bags set out on a bench. With only a nod, he moved to Tag's side and sorted through the items he'd accumulated through years of equipment changes. A few he'd bought at a military surplus store when he returned to the states. Some protection was better than none.

"Assuming a tracker is being used." Tag stuffed a loaded magazine into a pants pocket.

"Affirmative."

"Stationery?"

"Not at last check but nearby. In the mountains."

"Roger that." Tag angled his body. "Got no comms."

Beck let out a breath. "That's a tough lack to work

with. We'll stay close and maintain visuals." He glanced at his watch. Zero three fifty-five. "Dawn is at least two hours away."

For a moment, he reconciled the fact she'd have to remain a captive for that long. Probably scared out of her mind. Then he shoved away that concern and focused.

The last step was putting Tag's dog, Dex, and King into vests that resembled the ones they'd worn in combat. Beck didn't need King to track, but he felt most solid when they worked together. King's presence could be intimidating as hell.

"Are we clearing this plan with locals?"

Beck gritted his teeth. Tag was being too practical. "Hank called Barron, but he's just standing by. He hasn't been told the location."

"To keep our asses out of slings, we should head to his office first. Let the sheriff decide his next step."

Hands on hips, Beck confronted his friend. "You know we can do this as a two-man team. I hate like hell to waste the time."

Dark eyebrows crashed down. "Not wasted if we stay out of jail. I know where your head's at, believe me, buddy, I do. But we need to think locate and detain, not eliminate."

Twenty minutes later, Beck paced in the parking lot in front of the sheriff's office. "A dispute over a bad divorce. That's the man's reasoning? Most disagreements between exes don't end in armed abduction."

Tag crossed his arms over his chest. "Probably didn't help that you called him lazy."

Hank emerged through the door and shot a frown in Beck's direction. "Gunnar, you need work on your diplomacy." He gestured toward their parked vehicle. "Go and track the signal. Barron agreed to set up a vehicular block where the driveway intersects the state road. If capture isn't obtained, flush them in that direction. Depending on what goes down."

Beck tossed up his hands. "Finally." He took a big step toward the truck.

"Remember, the copter can't land, but from treetop level, the rotors and the spotlights instill fear in anyone escaping."

"I will." Beck nodded and patted his vest pocket where he'd stored the earpiece communicators Hank supplied. "Thanks, Hank."

During the drive along the winding road, Beck dialed down his mood from emotional hothead to level-headed tracker. The fact he let Tag drive his truck proved he was doing what he could to get control of his fear. He used the time to run over their plan as he focused on the blinking light on his phone. His only connection to Danae. "Less than a mile. How close should we go?"

"Not much farther. Our headlights will give away our approach if someone's on guard duty."

"Understood. Park the truck across the path. Make it one more deterrent."

"You sure?"

"Yeah, I can replace the truck. But I can't risk them getting away with Danae."

The pair worked their way up the rocky terrain, checking each other's position with their night-vision goggles and whispered comments. Both dogs stayed on task and stuck close.

Over the next rise, Beck spotted a square of light through the trees and flipped up his NVGs. A window in a cabin. About twenty feet of treeless ground surrounded the end of the structure. He side-stepped to Tag and handed him King's lead. "Let me recon the cabin and assess the next step. Going silent." He tapped the outside of the device in his right ear. "Back in less than five." As he moved away in a wide circle skirting the clearing, he heard a single whimper from King.

The first circuit verified no one stood watch at the lit windows. Based on the size of the building, it probably had four rooms, max. For the second circuit, he eased next to the structure's exterior walls and glanced in windows. No one in kitchen at the back. Two men in living room, both looked relaxed and possibly asleep. Pistols on coffee table. After rounding the front porch, he flipped down his NVGs to check the other side.

The blip on his phone screen showed Danae should be on this side of the cabin. In the second room, a faint green outline of a body showed in the middle of the bed. For a second, he closed his eyes to calm his heartrate. *I found her*. Keeping his gaze trained on the front door, he walked into the relative protection of the trees and worked his way over to Tag's position.

"As we thought, cabin is fueled with propane. Don't recognize the sedan parked near back door. Two bogies in front room, weapons nearby. Danae's on bed in the back west side bedroom." Inhaling, he hoped she hadn't been drugged. If she was, he'd have to carry her out. "Original plan will work. I'll shut off propane, call 'mark', and we breach the doors twenty seconds later. Once I have Danae outside, I'll give the all clear, and we meet at the truck."

"In and done in two minutes, max."

"Twenty bucks says I'm a hundred yards away in ninety seconds." He offered a fist, and they bumped knuckles to seal the bet. Winding the leash once more around his left hand, Beck straightened to a crouch and worked his way through the trees until the back of the cabin was straight ahead. One final time, he reviewed the actions—break cover to the propane tank, verify cabin went dark, mark to start countdown, zag to back step, wait out the count, then enter and seek his target.

The steps of the plan played out like ordered with no hitches. Seconds were lost when he whispered her name to let her know his identify and rested his cheek against hers to breathe in her orange-basil scent. He unsheathed the knife strapped to his calf and sliced through the duct tape on her ankles, torso, and wrists. Working a finger under her blindfold, he pushed it off her head.

King nosed her thigh and hip.

As soon as her hands were free, she grabbed at the tape strip over her mouth.

But he eased them away, brought them to his jaw, and shook his head. Removing it would hurt, and she'd need to recover. But they needed to be gone. With hands on her shoulders to orient her, he lifted a knee to her ass and nudged her toward the rear door.

To the count of two, he watched her stumble in that direction, bracing a hand on the wall. He backed down the narrow hallway, his weapon trained on the room where he heard muttered curses. Once through the back door, he holstered his weapon and anchored an arm around her back. Jogging past the propane tank, he unwound the lead to give King more freedom. "All clear."

Twenty seconds deeper into cover and past the tree line, he stopped and checked his watch. *Damn.* A minute forty. Tag won the bet. Beck turned to Danae, who sucked in breaths through her nose. Her green silhouette was the most beautiful sight he'd ever seen. He flipped up the NVGs then reached to one corner of the tape. "Removing this will hurt. You ready?"

The dim outline of her head nodded.

Grimacing, he ripped it off then cupped her face

with his hands and rained kisses over her lips and cheeks.

With a strangled sob, she threw herself against his chest. "You found me. How?"

"Later." He peeled off her grasp and set her away so he could grab her hand. "Run downhill. We're headed to my truck."

After her second stumble, he steered them to the side where he figured they'd find a packed trail. From there, he scanned the area and kept them going downhill. The familiar grind of an engine starting snagged his attention. In the next clearing, he spotted the outline of his truck. Tag had repositioned the vehicle so it headed downhill.

"Oh, thank God." Danae ran for the passenger door.

Beck led King to the back of the truck so he could jump up then set the tailgate in place. Just as Beck climbed inside, he heard an engine roar and saw headlights swing through the trees above. "They're on the move. Let's hope the sheriff is in place."

"He will be." Tag stomped on the accelerator and bounced the truck along the rutted road.

Beck stripped off the helmet and let it drop behind the seat. He stretched an arm over her shoulders and pulled Danae close. She trembled against his body, but all he cared about was that she sat beside him. He leaned down and lowered his voice. "Are you hurt?" Then he twisted his head hard left to hear her response.

"Just shaken."

In the east, the sky lightened to gray and threw the trees into relief. "Flash your lights so Barron knows we need to pass."

The space between the patrol cars widened, and Tag slowed the truck until he could steer through the gap.

As soon as the truck stopped, Beck was out and running to the sheriff's side. "Danae's safe. Two guys headed this way in a sedan. Both are armed."

"Glad your plan played out well. We've got the scene now until the FBI shows up."

Being dismissed in that way didn't sit well. He walked back to the truck but took up a position against the front bumper. With the sky brightening by the minute, he had a good-enough view from here. He wanted to make sure the guys were detained, so they couldn't come after her again.

Tag exited the truck and called to Dex. "Might as well see this through and join the welcoming party."

"Affirmative." He did want a front-row seat to see who had been tormenting her. "King, *komma*."

In an instant, the dog cleared the truck bed and was at his side.

Beck stooped to pick up the lead and headed toward the near end of the blockade. The bad guys didn't have to know these dogs weren't trained to attack. Soldier-dog teams presented a formidable sight. Especially when the ex-soldier half of this team was very pissed off.

He glanced at Tag, who responded with a curt nod. The success Beck had here in planning and executing the mission proved he and King could function almost like they had before.

The sedan barreled around the last curve in the road, sending rocks skittering against tree trunks.

"Light them up."

Bright spotlights from the patrol cars converged on the vehicle, displaying two shocked passengers.

Brakes screeched, and the back tires kicked up dust.

Through the loudspeaker came a deep command. "This is Sheriff Barron. Turn off the engine and exit the vehicle. Keep your hands in sight at all times."

Beck narrowed his gaze on the men who climbed out. Neither was Giles. He glanced over his shoulder toward the truck and saw Danae pushing open the truck door.

She walked, with both arms wrapped around her middle. "I need to see who's responsible."

"Sure." Nodding, he pulled her close and rubbed a hand up and down her arm. Night temperatures at this elevation got chilly, even in summer. "As soon as they're in cuffs."

A few minutes later, the sheriff approached and handed her a blanket. "Are you up to seeing if you know the men?"

"I most certainly am." Danae lifted her chin and met his gaze then stepped away. She wrapped the blanket over her shoulders and walked at the sheriff's side.

Protectiveness swelled. Beck wanted to follow but knew she would emerge stronger if she faced them on her own. He shifted his body to the best angle to catch their conversation, but the pair had moved too far away.

Until she yelled.

From what he heard, she recognized them and wasn't pleased.

With an arm around her waist, Sheriff Barron yanked her, kicking and flailing, from the side of the patrol car. Then he spoke into his shoulder radio.

Beck didn't wait for what the approaching deputy would say. "King, *häl*." He tightened the lead, jogged to her side, and pulled her into a loose hug. "Hey."

She stopped struggling.

His gesture was more containment than affection—although that emotion fought for supremacy. "So, I take it you know the kidnappers?" He smoothed a hand over her rigid back, making the blanket bunch and wrinkle.

Her eyes narrowed. "Nestor Spaneas and Stavros Mylonas. They're Giles' security team, but I've known them for four years." She tilted up her head and stared, her mouth drawn tight. "How could they scare me?"

He spotted the sheen in her eyes, and his throat tightened. "I'm sorry, Danae. Betrayal is never easy to understand."

King tugged against the lead, his nose lowered.

"Hang on." Beck released her then crouched and ran his fingers through King's neck fur. Under his touch, the dog tensed and trembled like before a mission. Could he be working a scent? Hope rose in Beck's chest. "King, *söka*." He loosened the lead so it could slip through his fingers.

King lunged toward the patrol car, his head swinging a few inches right and left. Then he laid flat on his belly, his nose pointed toward the shoes of the man inside.

"Hey, sheriff. Come look." Beck waited until the sheriff approached then pointed toward his downed dog. "King scented explosives of some type on this man." He couldn't keep the pride from his voice. *King is back*. "Could be the person who torched Danae's shed roof last night."

"A fire?" Barron's eyebrow rose. "Never heard about that incident."

Beck shrugged. "Everything happened so fast. I'm sure she intended to file a report today."

Nodding, the sheriff spoke into his shoulder radio. "Holmes, bring the evidence kit and a large bag."

"Are you satisfied these guys won't skip out of being charged?" She watched the scene then looked up to meet his gaze.

Tightening his hold, he gave a short nod. "The sheriff will want our statements. Do you feel up to doing that?"

Her body sagged. "I want to go home and fall asleep in your arms. Can we do that?"

He drew her close and set his chin on her head. *Home.* That word popped an immediate vision of her bedroom. He grinned. That idea suited him fine.

EPILOGUE

A MONTH LATER, Danae sat in an anteroom on the second floor of a Philadelphia courthouse. On another occasion, she might take note of the historic details of the carved wainscoting and wood panels. Instead, she fidgeted with the hem of the black skirt, wanting to be finished with her grand jury testimony regarding the flash drive.

Within moments of their arrival, Beck had been taken to a different room.

The realization they had barely been separated since the night she was abducted floated through her, providing a smidge of comfort.

The door opened. "Dr. Orestes, the jury will hear you now."

She stood and followed the clerk across the hall. From the corner of her eye, she saw the movement of an opening door and caught a glimpse of Beck, so handsome in a navy suit, exit the other side of the room.

He scanned the area and spotted her then grinned. He formed a fist, pounded it against his chest, and mouthed, *stay strong*.

Giving a nod, she marched into the room and took the seat facing filled chairs. From the first question the prosecuting attorney posed, she gave her answers in the same straight-forward way as she'd written in her note of discovery to the FBI. The scope of the charges against Giles vindicated her opinion.

Investigations had been underway for months, and the flash drive was the final piece needed to make the weapons smuggling and money laundering charges strong enough. Or at least, that interpretation was her best guess. The attorney who contacted her didn't say much besides telling her the proceedings were a way to get her written statement on the record.

When that ordeal was done, she walked through the door with her head held high then collapsed on the nearest bench.

Beck sat at her side and handed her a water bottle. "How was it?"

"The questioning went on forever." She gulped several sips. "Thanks."

He arched an eyebrow. "You were inside only ten minutes."

"Really?" She rolled her tight shoulders and

laughed. "Well, I'm glad that responsibility's over. Your testimony went okay?"

He nodded. "We've done our part. The legal system will do the rest."

Butterflies invaded her stomach but for a new reason. "Are you ready for the next showdown?"

"That's the word you use for a meal with your parents?" He glanced at his watch. "We still have almost an hour."

She jumped up. "That means we have to hurry so I can have a big glass of wine before they arrive. In my family, if you're not thirty minutes early, you're late."

Settled into the front seat of their rental car, she gazed out the window at the tall buildings along the downtown street. "I do miss seeing these sights." At the next intersection, she perked up and pointed across Beck's body. "We're passing my alma mater."

After a quick glance, he nodded then checked the navigation screen. "At least we're headed out of downtown so the traffic is loosening."

She sucked in a breath. "So, let's go over topics of acceptable conversation."

The light changed red. He turned his head. "Is this discussion necessary?"

"Absolutely." She reached for his hand and squeezed then brushed damp palms along her skirt. "Don't mention that you've officially changed your mailing address to mine." Why did she feel like she was the one meeting *his* parents?

"Okay." He focused forward and steered the car through the intersection.

"Or that on your last case, your team located an explosives cache that could have blown a hole in the Montana prairie the size of ten football fields cubed." She held up a hand. "Your words, not mine." At the next street, she glanced around to get her bearings. Only a couple blocks left.

She tightened her grip on the console. "Or that I was taken from my house at gunpoint."

"Danae…" He shot her a wide-eyed look. "I thought you said you cleared the air with your folks."

"I did, but mostly about the divorce. Once they learned about Giles and how he'd taken advantage of his position at the company, they forgave me for leaving him."

"That's big of them." He shook his head.

"For my family, the apology is a huge step." She drummed her fingers on the console between them.

The navigation system announced their destination was on the right. Beck paid the valet then escorted her into the restaurant.

Scents of olive oil and fennel tickled her nose.

A server walked by holding a plate with sizzling *souvlakia* and toasted pita bread.

Before they stepped up to the hostess, she turned and rested a hand on his lapel, hoping to absorb a bit of his strength. "This meal is the first time we've been face to face, and I want the experience to go well. With just the four of us, my μητέρα and πατέρας will have a chance to get to know you."

Smiling, he tapped her nose. "Grill me, you mean."

Rushing footsteps clattered behind them, and Danae peeked around Beck's shoulder and spotted her cousin. "What are you doing here?" A shiver ran over her skin. *They wouldn't have.* "Beck, my cousin Anezka. Actually, she's my cousin Dimitri's daughter." Danae touched Beck's chest. "Anezka, Beck Gunnar. He's my..." Crap, she hadn't rehearsed what term to use for him.

"Just call me her beau." He smiled and shook her hand.

Visions of the huge gathering she dreaded swam in her head. "I repeat, Anezka, why are you here? In this particular restaurant?"

"You know me, I'm always running late." She dashed forward and waved over her shoulder. "Sorry about spoiling the surprise."

They did. Danae sagged back against Beck. "If she's here, then waiting inside are probably another thirty or more of the local relatives." Secretly, she was thrilled at the family demonstration of accepting her back into the fold. But Beck had no preparation for her noisy, gregarious family. "Let me call and make our excuses."

"Why?" He settled a hand at her hip and turned her to face him. "We're here, and we've been seen." He shrugged. "So, the meal won't be only for four."

"Try more like ten times that number." She shook

her head, watching his expression for any sign of strain or panic. "To some they seem rude, but they're just curious and think everyone has the right to know every detail about you."

He pressed a quick kiss to her lips then connected with her gaze. "Danae, I survived a decade of military deployments. I can handle your family, sweetheart." He stepped forward and held out his hand. "I won't be deterred. Rangers lead the way."

Whirlwind

Challenges Met in <u>*Blue Collar*</u>, a Boys Behaving Badly
Anthology

All authors appreciate hearing how their artistic creations are received by readers. With so many titles available, standing out from the crowd takes a bit of extra effort. I would humbly appreciate you spending a few moments to give your honest opinion of this title by going either to the book page on Amazon or Goodreads and listing a short review.

ABOUT LAYLA CHASE

On a dare from a close friend, Layla Chase challenged herself to explore the steamier side of romance and discovered characters whose stories needed sharing. She writes contemporary and historical stories about strong personalities who know what they want...or rather, **who** they want, and set out to get it.

To connect with Layla on the web:

Website:
www.laylachase.com

Facebook:
http://www.facebook.com/layla.chase.52

Amazon Author Page:
https://www.amazon.com/author/laylachase

  facebook.com/layla.chase.52

  amazon.com/author/laylachase

ORIGINAL BROTHERHOOD PROTECTORS SERIES

BY ELLE JAMES

Brotherhood Protectors Series

Montana SEAL (#1)

Bride Protector SEAL (#2)

Montana D-Force (#3)

Cowboy D-Force (#4)

Montana Ranger (#5)

Montana Dog Soldier (#6)

Montana SEAL Daddy (#7)

Montana Ranger's Wedding Vow (#8)

Montana SEAL Undercover Daddy (#9)

Cape Code SEAL Rescue (#10)

Montana SEAL Friendly Fire (#11)

Montana SEAL's Bride (#12) TBD

Montana Rescue

Hot SEAL, Salty Dog

ABOUT ELLE JAMES

ELLE JAMES also writing as MYLA JACKSON is a *New York Times* and *USA Today* Bestselling author of books including cowboys, intrigues and paranormal adventures that keep her readers on the edges of their seats. With over eighty works in a variety of sub-genres and lengths she has published with Harlequin, Samhain, Ellora's Cave, Kensington, Cleis Press, and Avon. When she's not at her computer, she's traveling, snow skiing, boating, or riding her ATV, dreaming up new stories. Learn more about Elle James at www.elle-james.com

Website | Facebook | Twitter | GoodReads | Newsletter | BookBub | Amazon

Follow Elle!
www.ellejames.com
ellejames@ellejames.com

facebook.com/ellejamesauthor
twitter.com/ElleJamesAuthor